I0630720

HARLOW

THE HASTINGS SERIES #2

VANESSA SIENA

HARLOW

Copyright © 2020 by Vanessa Siena.
All rights reserved.
First Print Edition: February 2020

Limitless Publishing, LLC
Kailua, HI 96734
www.limitlesspublishing.com

Formatting: Book Pages By Design
Cover Design: Deranged Doctor Design

ISBN-13: 978-1-64034-811-0

No part of this book may be reproduced, scanned, or distributed in any printed or electronic form without permission. Please do not participate in or encourage piracy of copyrighted materials in violation of the author's rights. Thank you for respecting the hard work of this author.

This is a work of fiction. Names, characters, places, and incidents either are the product of the author's imagination or are used fictitiously, and any resemblance to locales, events, business establishments, or actual persons—living or dead—is entirely coincidental.

Dedication

To my Mom and my brother Luca, who will never read my books because Mom doesn't speak English and Luca doesn't really read. Or care. LOL. Love you!

CHAPTER ONE

Hunter

Having someone over was the last thing I wanted. I didn't feel comfortable enough to take girls here, knowing they'd be disgusted by the way I lived. That was poorly said and probably misunderstood. My trailer wasn't disgusting and I didn't have any mold. I kept my home clean, my clothes always perfectly folded, and every surface was shiny. I needed to feel comfortable in that small space and I knew it was enough for me. Yet, the few girls who came here some years ago all told me the same thing: The sex was amazing, but this place is creepy and ugly.

Those girls wanted something big. A huge house, a nice car, and money they could spend on themselves on a daily basis. If I didn't live in Hastings, and if I stopped working for Gunner, all they desired would've been possible for me to offer them.

Even if the girls I sometimes dated were hot and

interesting, I never felt the need to let them in on my secrets. I knew they weren't right for me. And even seeing them standing in my trailer I knew they just didn't fit in. My life didn't have any space for girls like them.

Seeing Harlow standing right there, in the middle of my home, looking around with a small, genuine smile on her lips was all I needed to realize that she was the one who fit. The moment she stepped inside, something in her eyes lit up. She looked almost fascinated by the small room I called my living room and kitchen. Her eyes wandered around and I took in her beauty, hoping her smile never faded, but grew bigger. We didn't speak, and I wondered what she was thinking. I kept my eyes on her, shoving my hands into my front pockets.

After some minutes, and after she finally settled her eyes on mine, her bottom lip got caught between her teeth and a bigger smile spread across her face. She didn't talk though, and I hoped I wasn't just blankly staring at her and making a fool out of myself. She then moved toward me, steady on her feet even after that horrible accident, and reached her arms around my waist. Her body pressed into mine and her head rested against my chest.

"It's even better than I imagined," she finally said. I smiled at that, lowering my head to kiss the top of hers, then taking my hands out of my pockets and lifting my arms to return her hug gently.

"Good. I like it too," I told her, happy about her never-ending positive attitude about everything. How could anyone not adore her?

I stroked her back and enjoyed having her back

in my arms. It felt like months that I hadn't held her like this. I felt myself relax the instant she touched me and I started to realize that she was my safe place. I felt calm with her next to me. Funnily enough, I always thought women could never make a man feel this way. I was so damn wrong. Growing up with the shit I went through and knowing no one really cared about me was fucking hard. I was a grown-ass man, yet I had no problem with accepting the fact that I found strength and joy thanks to a woman. No shame in that.

"I missed you." The simplicity in those words had a huge impact on me. We had seen each other just twelve hours ago and we both felt the same way. Hell, this was either going to end in heaven or hell.

Either way, as long as she'd be by my side, I'd be happy anywhere.

"I'm glad you're here," I told her, looking at her now and taking her face into my hands. "I'm not sure what you wanna do but I thought we could just talk. Stay in bed the whole day." I wasn't romantic, even if what I was thinking came close to it, but cuddling up in bed with her, the rain falling outside and thunder doing its best to sound as scary as possible sounded perfect to me.

"I like that idea." Her voice was still a bit raspy. I smiled at her response and studied her face for a second before lowering my head once again to kiss her. Her lips immediately moved against mine and the small moan escaping her made me want to pick her up and press her against the wall, making sure I'd hear more of those sweet sounds. I couldn't do that, though. Not yet. I had rushed things with her one too many times and I wanted to take it slow. I needed to explore her body with patience and—fuck me. I wasn't me anymore. How was I getting so fucking soft all of a sudden?

Harlow's tongue against mine made me come back from my new, confusing thoughts and I tried to concentrate on the kiss. I slid my tongue inside her mouth slowly, tasting her sweetness and trying not to hurt her with my hands traveling up and down her upper body. Her curves were beautiful. Her breasts felt amazing pressed against my chest, and the curves from her waist to her hips were impressive. I couldn't help myself, and my hands found their way to her ass, squeezing it just right. Another moan escaped her and I felt my cock react.

I didn't want it to get involved, but I guess there was no way around it. Harlow made me feel some type of way and I sure as hell wasn't going to ruin it.

I deepened the kiss, holding her closer than ever. Her hand came up to rest on my chest and the other came up to touch the side of my neck, letting her fingers brush through my hair. She tugged at the ends of it slightly, letting me know that she was enjoying this just as much as I was.

I felt a smile on her lips, her hand now taking a fistful of my hair at the back of my head and holding it tightly. "I like this," she said into the kiss, and I knew she meant my full head of hair. I've always caught the attention of others with my hair, but Harlow's was the only one that counted right now.

"Good," I murmured, wanting to say so much more, but I wasn't ready to let go of her yet.

CHAPTER TWO

Harlow

My heart was beating a thousand miles per hour and I was sure Hunter was the only one who could ever make me feel that way. The way he held my body close to him while he kissed me was incredible. I felt safe. Loved.

I was holding onto his hair and shoulder, making sure my knees wouldn't give in. The weakness I felt made me realize how big of an impact he had by just kissing me. I loved that about him and I hoped that feeling would never vanish.

Then there was something else urging me to go further than just making out in the middle of his home. The bulge in his pants told me that he was feeling excited too. I had pressed my hips against him more than once and I felt him move away every time. I wondered if he was doing it because he didn't like it, but then I thought, that's Hunter we're talking about here. And to be honest, I don't **think** any guy would ever reject a sign like that from a girl.

So why was he not letting me feel him against me? I knew he was getting erect. I knew what a boner was and I also knew that the way his breath hitched from time to time, that he was enjoying this too.

I tried once again, pushing more into his body and pressing my abdomen against his crotch. This time, I felt his cock was much harder and I smiled into the kiss, knowing I was the one making him feel that way.

"We gotta slow down, love." He broke the kiss, yet kept me close to him. I looked up, his eyes on mine with lowered lids and desire showing through them.

"Why?" I asked, feeling the need to pout like a little child. I was getting frustrated. I knew sex was something that needed to be taken one step at a time. But maybe sex wasn't what I wanted just yet. I just needed Hunter to touch me. Or let me touch him.

"Because my dick is damn close to exploding in my fucking pants and that's not something I would be proud of," he said in a chuckle and I bit down on my bottom lip and dropped my gaze, taking one small step back and looking at the bump in his pants.

"We're just kissing," I said, then looked back up into his eyes. "Yeah, we are. But you have no idea how much your sweet mouth can do to me."

A shiver came over me and I hoped he wasn't just saying that to get me off of him. Or was I just interpreting it all wrong?

"Can I touch it?" I asked, looking down again. Hunter didn't answer at first and I was scared to look at his face. I didn't want him to get mad or push me away.

His head lowered and his lips kissed my cheek. He whispered, "If you're gonna start this, I'll finish it. But I'm not sure I can do that without hurting you."

I wasn't hurting that much. I had bruises around my upper body and I knew whatever we would've done would involve him grabbing my waist or hips. Funny how I thought about him fucking me when I never even had such an experience.

Yet, him having a boner was one thing I could deal with easily without him touching me. "Isn't that uncomfortable?" I looked back into his eyes, seeing a glimpse of amusement in them. His hands came up to cup my face once again, then he pressed a kiss to the tip of my nose.

"It's the worst feeling ever," he said, then a smug grin appeared on his face. "Tell me what you're thinking, Harlow."

I let my eyes travel over his face, then shrugged. He knew where I was going with it. And I was ready to try something new.

"Maybe I could help you with it," I said, my voice now sounding much smaller. He kept his gaze locked on mine and that stupid grin grew. I felt my cheeks warm up and he knew damn well what he was doing to me by making me say things like that.

"Not sure what you mean, love. How'd you like to help me exactly?" he teased. I rolled my eyes at him, then took a deep breath, making sure I'd sound as serious as possible.

"Maybe I can touch it."

I knew Hunter was close to letting out a laugh but he was holding it back. "With *it*, you mean…" he started and I pressed my lips together. Why was I making such a big deal out of it? It was a normal thing. People did it all the time.

"Your cock." There. I said it. And it wasn't half as bad as I thought. Hunter's eyes looked pleased with my answer and I let out a breath, releasing all my frustration.

A smile touched his lips now and he reached for my hand, slowly leading it to his pants. The moment my hand covered his cock, I looked down and was surprised at just how hard it actually felt. It felt big too. Though, I didn't really have anyone to compare him to.

Hunter let his hand fall to his side and with the other, he grabbed a fistful of my hair at the back of my head and softly kissed my forehead. "I'm not pushing you to do this, all right? Stop if you don't wanna go any further."

I nodded slowly, moving my hand over his rigid cock. Every time I carefully squeezed, his hand pulled at my hair just as gently. I couldn't look up at him and I wanted to see more of him.

"Can you take this off?" I asked, meaning his pants, and returning his glance. He nodded once but left his hands where they were.

"You do it," he instructed, and like a little kid opening a present, my hands flew to his zipper and quickly opened it. With my fingers gripping the waistband of his pants, I pushed them down, leaving

9

him standing there in just his shorts. I could see the size of his cock now that just a thin layer of fabric was covering it. Impressive.

I covered it with my hand again, giving it a light squeeze and then looking up at his face. He was watching me, his tongue darting out to wet his lips.

"Here," he said in a whisper, and covered my hand with his and squeezed hard. "Just like that. Up and down."

I smiled at the way he showed me what he liked. I felt more comfortable with that and knowing what made him felt good was a step forward for me.

He let go of my hand again, letting me touch him the way he told me to. A small groan escaped him and I felt a spot on his shorts turn wet. I quickly looked up in surprise.

"Just precum, love." He smiled at me, lowering his head to kiss my lips softly. "It feels amazing," he murmured into the kiss and I couldn't help but grin.

I was enjoying this. Too much.

CHAPTER THREE

Hunter

I couldn't take it any longer standing up. I needed to sit down and watch sweet Harlow moving her small hand up and down my length. My shorts were still on, but it was the best feeling ever. Almost as if she was teasing me. Last time a girl touched me like that was some months ago and having Harlow doing this for the first time made it all feel a thousand times better.

"Come here." I took her hand off my cock, pulling her toward my bedroom. It wasn't big, but it fit a double bed perfectly. I sat down at the end of it, looking up at her. She took in the small room, smiling. When her gaze came back to mine, she looked a little lost. Her hand reached down to my shorts, though, and I knew she wasn't going to keep it like that.

"I don't really know what to do now," she told me quietly and that made me grin a little too much. Too damn sweet.

11

Her hand grabbed my cock again and I let out a groan, knowing I was closer than I should've been. She was doing so little, yet her actions made me feel all weak and ready to shoot my load.

"If I tell you what I like, will you try?" I asked, hoping I wasn't going to scare her off. I had a dirty mouth. No denying that. But she was so damn innocent.

"Yes." Her simple answer made me want to beat on my chest like King Kong.

"On your knees," I told her, nodding to the spot in front of me. I had my legs slightly parted so she would fit in perfectly, allowing her access to my dick, which was heavily pulsating and wishing for a release.

Harlow didn't hesitate. She knelt in front of me, her eyes falling onto my erection now and then. I took in the view, taking a picture in my head to remember this sight forever. She was so fucking gorgeous.

"Okay if I take these off?" I asked, pointing to my shorts. She shook her head quickly, excitement dancing in her big eyes. I was sure it would be the first time she'd seen one in person. I was glad I was her first.

I wasn't hurrying this though. The way she watched me as I pulled down my shorts was making me more and more excited for her to see.

As I took them off fully, I put them next to me on the bed, keeping my eyes on her face and grabbing my hardened cock in my left hand, slowly moving it.

Fuck me, I could definitely come by just

watching her watch me.

Her eyes, however, never really looked at it. A grin appeared on my lips and I couldn't help but chuckle. "You gonna look at it, love?"

Harlow's eyes slowly moved from mine down to my chest, then to my stomach, and finally, her eyes widened as they got to my cock. Without saying a word or warning me, her hand came up and wrapped around my base, slowly massaging my length up and down. I moved my hand, and I was surprised by how brave she was by just doing what she did.

"Fuck, just like that."

***

Harlow

His moans were enough for me to know that he was enjoying the way I moved my hand around his cock. Hunter was now leaning back, keeping his upper body up with his elbows behind him on the bed. His eyes were watching my every move and I wanted him to tell me what other things he liked.

I wasn't sure how to ask him if he wanted a blowjob, though. That was a weird thing to ask a guy, right?

"Can I, uh, can I try to..." I hated the fact that I was too shy to ask him if he wanted a blowjob, but I wasn't too shy to just grab his dick after seeing it for the first time.

"I want your pretty mouth around my cock, love, now."

Thankful for his words, I pressed my lips together and thought about how to approach this whole thing. Literally. It was huge.

I looked back up at Hunter with an awkward smile and a laugh erupted from his chest.

"Fucking hell," he murmured, then bent over to kiss me before looking back into my eyes. "Do you even have any damn clue how fucking stunning you are?"

I couldn't answer that question and I wasn't sure he even wanted an answer to that. I gave him a smile, this time a real one. "Just start slow. Tip to base. I'm positive you'll make it feel like heaven."

I looked back at his cock, slowly lowering my head and closing my eyes as my lips parted and closed again around the tip. I immediately tasted something salty, knowing it's the precum.

"Fuck!" he groaned and grabbed a fistful of my hair at the back of my head. I felt him lightly pushing down on it, making me open my mouth wider and taking in more of his length.

"Just like that. Slow and easy, love." Not sure why, but knowing he was enjoying this made me feel empowered. He had made me feel good before and I was happy to return his favor.

I knew teeth weren't really a turn on while doing something like that so I tried my best not to hurt him, instead, I used my tongue more to lick him while I slowly started to move my head up and down.

"Yes, baby. Use that tongue," he encouraged through gritted teeth and I felt the heat between my thighs grow.

I kept on moving my head, taking his cock in as much as I could and sucking at the tip every time. I wasn't sure I was doing it right, but he seemed to like it.

I still felt the need to try something else and so I took him in further, getting to know that gag reflex I knew existed. It didn't bother me as much, though. I took him deeper into my mouth, moving my hand at the base and squeezing, making him moan over and over again.

"If you keep on doing that, love, I'm gonna come soon."

Good. That was sort of what I was going for.

CHAPTER FOUR

Harlow

I felt his dick throb and his fist grabbed my hair tighter at the back of my head. His groans told me that he was keeping something in, resisting the urge to come. I took that as an approval. He liked what I was doing, and I wasn't going to lie to myself; I liked it too.

"Fuck, love," he said under his breath. "That view I have is incredibly hot. You're fucking beautiful with those lips of yours around my cock." Hearing him say those words sparked something in me and I now knew how beautiful doing things like this was when you did it with someone you loved.

I opened my eyes, looking up at him while I still moved my head up and down, letting him guide me with his hand in my hair. His eyes were full of lust, his lips slightly parted, and when he realized I was looking at him, his tongue darted out to wet his lips.

"Shit, sweetheart. Keep looking at me with those eyes and I won't be able to keep it in any longer."

Those words did something to me and my goal now was to see him come. I wasn't sure how I felt about his semen in my mouth, but I also wasn't sure how to tell him not to come in my mouth. I had tasted his precum and it was salty. That wasn't really the bad part. I just wasn't sure I would like the thought of having sperm in my mouth. It just didn't sound good to me.

"Fuck," he murmured before a small grin appeared on his lips. "I know what you're doing." I was keeping my eyes on his. "Teasing me with those eyes." He ran his other hand through his hair.

I tried to smile, because with a cock in my mouth that was kind of difficult, but the idea of it was present. When I kept blowing and stroking his cock, I could tell he wasn't going to last a minute longer. His hand reached for his cock and his other pulled my head up. "Keep on doing that," he said while my hand was still moving up and down his length. I still wasn't sure what to do about the cum situation.

"Just hold it up toward my stomach." He must've seen how worried and confused I was since he just answered me by reading my thoughts. I nodded, knowing his cum would stain his shirt. My hand was still moving and his eyes were closed before he said, "I'm gonna come, fuck!"

And with that, white fluids covered his stomach, his cock pulsating, and a deep groan coming from his mouth. He put his hand over mine, slowing me down and looking back at me with a satisfied grin.

***

Hunter

The way her eyes showed me all types of emotions was amusing. There was surprise, satisfaction, and curiosity in them and all that mixed with her swollen lips and red cheeks was a sight I wanted to see every damn day.

When I was sure I was able to let go of my dick and the orgasm was over, I sat back up straight, cupping her face into my hands and kissing her softly. Her lips moved against mine without hesitation and her hands came up around my neck.

I lifted her to straddle my lap so she wouldn't have to kneel anymore and my arms wrapped around her back. Just as the kiss was getting deeper, she backed up and took a deep breath, then smiled at me.

"Your shirt is messy now," she told me, looking down between us. My cock was still exposed, still quite erect for just releasing a load.

"Let me go change." I gave her another kiss, lifting her again to put her down next to me. "Get under the covers. I'll be right back."

I walked back to the front of the trailer, picking up my pants from the floor and then entering the bathroom to throw them into the basket with dirty clothes. I took off my shirt too, then cleaned myself with a wet cloth. Her heat around my cock felt amazing but I was ready to get into bed with her and just hold her close.

Before going back to the bedroom, I went to the kitchen to grab a glass of water, bringing it back to the bedroom and handing it to Harlow. She took it while eyeing me, letting her gaze wander all over my naked body. I grinned, grabbed a pair of shorts from the drawer, and a shirt from my closet and putting them on.

"You don't have any tattoos," she said, putting the now empty glass onto the bedside table. I crawled under the covers next to her, lying back and taking her with me. She cuddled up to me, her eyes on mine again.

"I don't. Not sure I need any. Aren't really my style."

She smiled, her hand coming up to touch my cheek. "I like you the way you are," she whispered.

I kissed her forehead, pulling her even closer. "You're adorable," I told her and returned her gaze.

"Does your brother know you're here?"

She nodded. "He gave me a ride here."

So Jagger was okay with her being here. I was sure we had settled this at the hospital but I could also understand his concerns.

"What did Bliss tell you when we were gone last night?"

Her lips pressed into a thin line and her eyes left mine. She looked like she was almost scared to tell me what my sister told her.

Great. I guess Bliss just let out everything about me and my damn past.

"Not much. I mean…" she sighed, playing with a strand of hair at the back of my head. "She told me a bit about you. What you went through. And how you grew up. She didn't tell me a lot. I'd much rather hear it from you. When you're ready, that is."

I studied her face for a while, knowing I would

tell her someday.

She was giving me time to reflect on it but since Bliss already started it all, I could finish it.

CHAPTER FIVE

Hunter

Having her back in my arms, knowing she wouldn't be leaving, gave me the strength to talk about my past. I always wanted to tell her, let her into my thoughts and let her know that I wanted her not only close physically but also mentally. Harlow told me that Bliss had told her some things, but she wasn't very specific. I didn't believe that Bliss didn't tell a whole lot, but I knew Harlow wanted to hear it all from me.

She knew it was a tough story and the memories I still carried around were not pretty. Harlow, and the sweet, big-hearted soul she was, knew that it meant a lot to me to tell her my side of it all. Once again, she had shown me how incredibly kind and selfless she was.

Her eyes were on mine the whole time and she was patiently waiting for me to start talking. Every now and then a small smile touched her lips, letting me know I should take my time. My thumb caressed her cheek, my nose touching hers briefly before I kissed her lips softly. She moved her lips against mine and I realized we had time. Nothing was going to bother us and we could spend the day being lazy and enjoying each other's company. Just what I wanted.

It was almost lunchtime and I never really asked her if she had something to eat before coming here. "Are you hungry?" I asked after breaking the kiss. Her brows furrowed for a second, then a giggle escaped her.

"Are you trying to change the subject?" she asked back, smiling at me.

"I promise I will tell you my whole story. I just need to collect some thoughts and I wasn't sure if you had eaten yet."

She shook her head, licking her lips. "I had breakfast with Jagger this morning." That meant she had eaten around seven-thirty.

"I got some chicken and veggies. You good with that?" I got up from the bed, leaving her lying there with her body twisted in my sheets. Not sure I was going to ever wash those again. Her scent lingered in them and I knew I was going to sleep so damn good tonight.

The sight of her like that made me want to jump back into bed, keep her tightly in my arms and never leave.

Fuck, if she only knew what she was doing to me she might have some mercy on me.

"Sounds good to me," she said with a smile and sat up. "Do you want me to cook though?" I couldn't help but grin. "Why? You think I can't cook?"

She shrugged. "Can you?"

"Ouch." I put my hand over my chest, giving her a hurt look. "Damn, love. That hit something in my heart really hard." Of course, I wasn't serious. I let out a laugh to let her know I wasn't taking her prejudice serious.

"I'm sorry," she said and frowned. "I just never really met a guy who cooks. Jagger's a horrible cook. I shouldn't have judged."

I bent down to kiss her wrinkled nose, then shook my head at her. "It's okay." I stood back up. "I like to cook. Done it ever since I don't live with Bliss anymore. Calms me down in a way."

She nodded with a small smile, then got out of the bed. "I wanna watch you."

***

Harlow

He was procrastinating. I wasn't really hungry. The eggs and bacon this morning pretty much filled me up. But Hunter needed time and I would give that to him. So, watching him cook was what I did.

I sat on the counter, watching him cut the veggies and cook the meat. Every so often he would come over, kiss me passionately, then return to the stove. It was interesting to watch someone like Hunter cook. He was so concentrated, making sure the chicken breasts weren't going to burn and seasoning the veggies in the pan with more herbs than I expected him to have in his tiny home.

He fascinated me more and more and I knew there were more things I had yet to find out about him. Just like he did about me.

"What's your favorite food?" I asked, letting my legs dangle.

"Herb crusted rack of lamb. It's pretty expensive so I don't have it often," he told me.

"Why not?" I puckered my lips, thinking about the next sentence I wanted to say. "Don't you have just as much money as Jagger?"

He stopped for a second, then turned to me. "People at the store will think I'm some sort of thief getting a rack of lamb. So I send Bliss to get it for me but she's not really known around the city to have a lot of money, either. People know she's my sister and they assume she's just as poor as I am. Besides, the things we like shouldn't be taken for granted just because we have the money for it."

He had a point. I smiled at him and nodded to approve of what he just said.

"Do you like lamb?" he then asked and leaned back against the counter opposite of me.

I shrugged. "I never had lamb before. Jagger and I like to buy chicken and sometimes beef."

"Would you try it if I tell Bliss to get some racks? You'll love it."

"Sounds good to me," I told him.

"And maybe we let Jagger and Bliss come eat some too."

"I think that's a good idea."

Hunter wanting to let my brother and his sister be part of this made my heart feel even warmer than before. He wasn't hiding me from them and he wasn't hiding whatever we were from them, either.

We didn't have many people around us who we called family. Knowing that Hunter wanted to keep them close was amazing and I couldn't wait to sit around a table with them, deepening my relationship with Hunter and the new friendship I knew Bliss and I would have in the future.

CHAPTER SIX

Harlow

We had dinner and I enjoyed it a little too much. Hunter's cooking was amazing and he was very skilled. I had to give it to him. My cooking was okay. I mean, Jagger ate whatever I put on the table and that's what counted. But Hunter knew what to do to make a meal taste like one at a restaurant.

"Have you ever thought about working as a cook? I mean there are many restaurants around town that need people in their kitchens. Frankie needs more cooks too. Maybe you could get a job at the diner," I suggested, thinking it would be a nice idea working at the same diner with Hunter.

He let out a chuckle and shook his head. "I can barely keep my hands and eyes off you when you're around. How do you expect me to work and concentrate there with you running around with that short uniform on, hm?"

My cheeks felt hot, and even after giving him a blowjob and not feeling any shame in it, him giving

26

me compliments still made me feel silly and all tingly inside.

"I know you're trying to help, Harlow, but I don't want to work. Well, not like that."

My brows furrowed and I watched his face as he stood up, taking both our plates and putting them into the sink. "What's it like?" I asked.

"What's what like?" he asked back, glancing over his shoulder.

Pressing my lips together, I thought about how to put my thoughts into words that wouldn't come off offensive. "What's it like to…kill someone?"

He didn't move, his eyes still on mine, and I could tell by the way they showed me the emotions running through them that his mood was changing in an instant. Shit. Why would I even ask that?

"Why'd you think that I killed someone before?" he asked and turned, leaning back against the counter. I shrugged, puckering my lips and wishing I would've just been quiet for once. I couldn't take his stare anymore, so my hands were the next best option to look at.

"Harlow."

His voice was lower, almost like a growl. I didn't look up, furrowing my brows even more. "Don't be all shy now, love. You started this conversation, so we're having it."

**

Hunter

She shook her head and I tried to keep in all my

anger. I hated the way I made her feel when she shouldn't be feeling bad at all. I was the bad guy here and she had all the rights in the world to ask me about shit like that. So getting mad wasn't an option. But even if it was Harlow, I hadn't managed to keep my anger under control yet. I was trying my best.

"I don't wanna talk about it," she whispered, looking up at me with fear in her eyes and quickly looking back down. Fuck.

"Harlow," I repeated, taking a few steps before crouching down in front of her. I grabbed her hands with one of mine and with the other, I lifted her chin so she would have to look at me.

"I'm trying really hard here to make this work with us and I know I wasn't really good to you in the beginning. But the things you don't know yet are pretty hard to swallow. I want to tell you everything but I also don't want you to run because you're scared of me. That's the last thing I want, love."

It all sounded so wrong. I was a fucking killer, not sure if she knew about it or just guessed, but her brother was the same and I had to make sure that she wouldn't run.

"Remember me saying we gotta take this step by step?" I asked, slightly relieved that she was looking at me again. She nodded at my question, squeezing my hands.

"Good. I want to tell you every little detail so you can reflect on it and not just add things to my story with your imagination."

"So why don't you tell me now? I mean, I'm

imagining the worst scenarios in my head already so why can't you just tell me now?" she asked with a small voice.

Damn. She had a fucking point there.

I let out a sigh and let my head fall, closing my eyes. After a little while, I looked back up at her. "You made the killing thing up, right? Jagger didn't tell you about shit like that."

"No," she said slowly. "But now I know that I wasn't wrong about the killing thing."

This girl was showing me the smart side of her I hadn't seen before. I knew she wasn't stupid. She had brains. But right now, she was making me look like a fucking idiot. I was also getting nervous knowing I was about to tell her some of my deepest secrets.

"Don't be scared of me," I told her, just wanting to make sure she would still trust me.

"I'm not scared of you, Hunter. I just need some clearance. I know what you'll tell me won't be something anyone would just listen to and not call the police. But you and Jagger are both in it and I'd be stupid if I would snitch on my brother. Or the one I love."

Her last word surprised us both. Her eyes grew wide and I felt my mouth open and closing multiple times before a huge grin spread on my face, not able to hide it. "With 'the one you love' you meant Jagger…" I said, almost sarcastically.

She tensed, her whole face now turning red and her eyes leaving mine to look back at her hands. "No," she mumbled, rolling her eyes before looking at me. "God, I'm so embarrassed." Her hand came up to cover her eyes. She just admitted to loving me and all I wanted to do was say it back to her. But this was too fucking cute.

"I mean, it's a nice compliment," I said, still grinning. She sighed and uncovered her eyes to hit my shoulder with that hand. "Hunter…" she said with a pout and I enjoyed her embarrassed look a little too much.

I chuckled, cupping her face with both hands and moving closer to her. "I'm kidding." I kissed the tip of her nose before covering her mouth with mine. She didn't kiss me back at first but melted into the kiss after I stood back up and lifted her to her feet too. I wrapped my arms around her waist, pulling her close and feeling her hands wander up toward my neck.

"I love you too, Harlow."

It should've felt rushed. It should've taken us more time to know that we shared the same strong feelings for each other but it didn't. Even after this short amount of time, we knew it was right. No matter if I was about to tell her my darkest secrets and no matter what the future would hold for us, letting each other know how we felt came first.

CHAPTER SEVEN

Hunter

I held her in my arms for a while and just breathed in her scent, feeling both our hearts beat at the same pace and driving me crazy simultaneously because I never felt my heart beat that fucking fast. It almost felt like adrenalin. Telling her I loved her and knowing she felt the same wasn't something I thought I needed. Up until now, love wasn't really a thing I was too excited about. I had relationships before, sure. But with Harlow, I felt for the first time what it really meant to be in love with someone. I was slightly cringing at my own thoughts for being so fucking pussy whipped, but it was all just going up from now on.

"Are we moving too fast?" she asked in a whisper against my chest and I looked down at her.

"Hm?"

She turned her head to look up at me. "Are we doing this whole thing too fast? I feel like falling in love takes time," she said, unsure of her words. I frowned at her, shaking my head.

"Does it feel right to you?" I asked. "Are you having any doubts about us?"

She quickly shook her head and smiled at me with a sweet smile. "Not one doubt."

"Me neither. And I promise you, sweetheart," I started, kissing her lips softly before continuing, "I won't be going anywhere. You got me all wrapped up around your little finger."

Her smile grew at my cheesy words and a laugh escaped her. "This is a disaster." I knew she didn't mean that and that what we had was indeed a little disaster. We started out with me being a total dick toward her and a short time later I was telling her that I loved her.

"Do you really think you can keep up with me?" I asked. I was a handful. My anger wasn't under control and the littlest things triggered me. Somehow, though, knowing Harlow loved me made that anger go away. For the moment, at least.

"I kept up with you for the past few weeks. I think I can handle whatever is coming my way."

I believed her, yet I didn't want to hurt her again.

I studied her face long enough to realize that what she was saying was the truth. She deserved so much more. I wanted to give her more.

"Let's get comfortable. I wanna tell you everything."

"Are you sure?" she asked.

"What? Are you having doubts now?" I joked, smirking at her.

Her nose wrinkled and she shook her head

quickly. "No. I'd love to listen to your story."

***

Harlow

We sat on the small couch in his living room and turned to face each other, my legs pulled up underneath me to sit more comfortably. The beginning of his story was almost identical to what Bliss had told me. There were some things he added to the story about the way he felt and what his thoughts were about. I listened carefully, not wanting to miss anything. It was heartbreaking to hear his story and I wished somebody would've taken better care of baby Hunter and Bliss. They were both just kids, getting put through rough things early in life.

"Bliss was my rock. After every outburst of rage I had, she was the one pulling me back to earth and calming me down. When I was little I wasn't really sure where all that anger came from. I thought something was wrong with me. Well, there is something wrong with me. But I had to accept the fact that I wasn't the one carrying all the fault for it around. The people who tried to raise me were the ones making my brain go all wild and dizzy. I know that now. But that issue grew with me and that's why I was an ass around you."

He took a small break from talking, thinking about the things he wanted to say next. I reached for his cheek, patting it softly and running my thumb over his stubbled jaw. "I can imagine how hard it was for you to wrap your thoughts around that. And I've seen the worst of you. At least, I think that was the worst. But even if I'm wrong, I won't judge you for who you are."

"See, love," he said in a chuckle. "That," he said, pointing at me with his finger. "That's one fucking reason why everyone adores you. You're too damn kind. And I know I don't deserve you." He shook his head and I smiled at him. "I really hope you don't ever change your mind because I will keep you forever. Not gonna let you go anymore."

"Good, 'cause I won't leave."

"Good thing we got that settled." He grinned at me once more before getting back to his story.

"When I was sixteen, Bliss and I moved here, to Hastings. She was eighteen then and was able to take care of me on her own. She got the job at the diner she still works at and I tried to find a way to make my own money. I didn't know what work really was. I didn't have any education besides middle school and I wouldn't have gotten a job that would pay me good money. I was on the streets a lot. I met people my age but I most times went back home with a bloody nose. I couldn't keep away from fistfights. It was something I was good at and it just felt right. Time passed and people started to avoid me. They knew I was trouble and I was known as the outsider. Always around town on my own, dirty clothes and bruises all over my face and arms. I knew I was safe that way and no one would even try to get close to Bliss. That's when our roles switched. I became her protector.

"At eighteen, Bliss told me to stop fucking

around and get a job. What she didn't know was that I had one. I sold drugs to high school kids and since they were pretty damn naïve I ripped them off every time. I had my money, but I wouldn't spend it on anything but food. Bliss found out about the drugs and that was the first time she ever showed me how brutally serious she could get. Almost scared the shit outta me. I explained to her that a normal job wasn't going to cut it for me. I needed something exciting and different. We were up all night discussing the ups and downs of being a drug dealer. She knew I wasn't going to give in so she tried to figure out the best way to let me do what I wanted without being scared something would happen to me. After a long talk, she made me promise not to do anything stupid."

Hunter paused and I let all of what he just said sink in. For now, everything he said wasn't that bad. It was an interesting story and the fact that he didn't go to high school never really showed in any way. Hunter was smart. Street smart, as Jagger would say.

But then, we all were. We knew our ways around life without any guidance from books or teachers in school.

We didn't need that. All we needed were people who stuck to us, no matter what.

CHAPTER EIGHT

Harlow

I was all ears for the next part of his story. I was kinda excited, but not in a positive way. I just really needed to know about the killing. He wasn't very secretive when I asked him about it some minutes ago so I knew something bad would come. But no matter what he said, I would sit and listen, accept it, and just push it aside. I knew Hunter was a good guy at heart. Jagger too. And if both of them ever had to kill someone to protect themselves, then it would be okay.

All of that still sounded crazy. But my life was normal and so I just had to accept whatever was coming.

"Are you still with me?" he asked with a smile and I nodded.

"Yes," I told him, reminding myself that I had to go apologize to Bliss for being a bitch the last time I saw her. I was rude to her and kinda kicked her out of my house for trying to help and explain the situation.

"I've mentioned Gunner before. He's our boss. Initially, we just sold drugs and guns. When he realized people wanted more than just those two things he started to import ammunition. His business quickly went through the roof and he knew he could make way more. He had people asking him for help to catch deceivers and people who messed with them. At first, Jagger and I weren't into that. We didn't want to mess with others and selling was something we were good at. We kept the selling business running while others started to go after people who owed others. But one night, one of our guys got killed and that's when Gunner found out that he wasn't the only one doing business like that. There was another guy, Kai, going against us, sending his people to kill ours."

"To kill your guys who were going after the ones who owed someone who paid them to do so," I said, hoping I was understanding all of it correctly. It was confusing. But I wanted to understand.

Hunter chuckled and nodded. "Something like that. Long story short; Kai sent his guys to kill Gunner's for killing people. Fuck, that's complicated, but stick with me, all right?" I nodded and braced myself for the next part. He was already talking about killing, which suddenly made me nervous. I wasn't nervous before but knowing there were multiple people going around town murdering others was starting to make me a little insecure. I loved walking alone at night after work and now I finally understood why Hunter insisted on taking me home at night. He was just trying to protect me.

Though, I wasn't sure what I had done wrong in life to get killed by some random guy in the middle of the night.

"After we lost one of our guys, Gunner told us to step up or leave. He wanted more people to work as hitmen. He offered us more than half the money people paid for us to kill someone. I can't tell you who those people are, but they pay a shit ton of money for just one hit." He stopped talking again, eyeing me carefully. "What are you thinking right now?" he then asked with a shy smile and I shrugged.

"I appreciate you telling me all this, but I think I just want to know how many there were," I said, returning his gaze. "How many you killed, I mean."

***

Hunter

Lying wasn't going to work. If Jagger ever opened up like that to her and told her exactly how many we killed, she'd know I lied since Jag and I did the jobs together. We split the money we got. We could be selfish and do some of the jobs alone, but we wanted to be safe. Make sure no one would be after us while we were after somebody else. Better safe than sorry.

"Fifteen." I watched her face for a reaction but all I got was a small nod. This girl was one of a kind.

"Have you ever gotten hurt? Or failed?"

I wasn't sure I heard her correctly. Instead of

fear, there was some sort of curiosity in her eyes. Every other person would've gotten sweaty hands and taken several steps back, but Harlow? Fuck me. That girl just knew who she could trust.

Even if the situation was weird, going from a hell of a blowjob to eating lunch, then confessing our love for each other before talking about killing people, I realized this was just who we were. We had ups and downs, and no matter what, we still needed each other's company.

"Never been hurt badly. And yeah, we failed several times." I smiled again, brushing a strand of hair from her cheek and tugging it behind her ear. "Is there something else you wanna know?"

She studied me for a while, then slowly shook her head. "Not really. I just don't want you or Jagger to get hurt."

"We won't. Trust me on that."

"So, Bliss knows all of that too, right?" she asked. I nodded.

"Do you think she's mad at me for telling her to be quiet that night? I feel horrible." And just like that, whatever I just told her about being a fucking hitman was accepted and put to the side and the next topic came up.

I let out a chuckle, shaking my head and trying to wrap my thoughts around her beautiful soul. How on earth did she stay so calm?

"She's not mad. You were put in front of a difficult situation and you had some anger in you. She's fine. She can handle a small outburst like yours. I mean, she kept up with my bullshit all her life."

Harlow laughed and shrugged. "I just wanna tell her I'm sorry."

"We can get dinner at the diner tonight. She's working."

"Sounds good to me. I'll let Jagger know to meet us there after work."

I nodded and she got up to get her phone from her tote bag, typing in a message to her brother. I watched her standing there, letting my eyes wander up and down her body and leaning back to enjoy the view. Her body was amazing.

Her smile caught my attention and she put her phone back down to walk over to me. I pulled her down on my lap, making her straddle me. "He said he will be there," she told me and I managed to give her a small nod before taking her mouth.

Not sure how, but I had to keep her in this trailer forever.

CHAPTER NINE

Hunter

I knew how important it was to Harlow to keep her brother close, even if I now was a part of her too. I wasn't taking that from her and I'm sure Jagger would not let me get away with it anyway. I couldn't take another beating from him. Hell, my nose was still a bit sore.

But I was planning on spending more time with Harlow. I had told her about my past now and even if I knew there wasn't much I didn't know about her since Jagger told me about their past before, I wanted to hear it from her. I knew she went through hell because of Dean, and never really knowing her mother was definitely not something she just forgot about.

I didn't know my parents either and I knew I would never get to meet them even if I tried looking for them. But then, I wasn't really sure I needed to know who those people were. It didn't feel like a good idea. Just thinking about having parents made me angry and the thought of looking into their eyes left me cold-hearted.

I think it was different for Harlow. Even if she never talked about Dean or her mother, I knew there was something inside of her wanting to make it all right. Hell, sweet Harlow would probably forgive her father for abusing her as a kid. I sometimes wondered if she knew what hate was. If there was something inside her mind letting her know there were bad people on this earth or if she only saw the good in people. Sure, her father probably wasn't good in any way, but Harlow would dig as deep as possible to find just one little thing that was good enough for her to forgive him.

If that day ever came and I'd have to watch her do just that, I wouldn't be able to sit there. That man had damaged and terrorized a small child's innocent life and now had the gall to come crawling back as if nothing ever happened. Same with Jagger.

"What are you thinking?" Harlow asked in a sweet voice, her eyes concerned and her hands brushing through the hair at the back of my head. She was still straddling me, my hands on her thighs and squeezing them lightly to let her know everything was fine.

"Nothing. Just remembered something." Lying wasn't necessary, but I knew I wasn't going to start this conversation about her father after the amazing day we had so far. It had gotten late and the rain finally stopped. It was foggy outside and the light shining through the window came from a streetlamp right in front of my trailer.

"It's five. We should probably head out to the diner. You ready? Or do you need to go change?" I asked her. She pushed out her bottom lip, looking down at herself and then shaking her head. "No, I think I'm good. Or do you think I should?"

I never observed her clothing choices before since her beauty distracted me from anything else. This time, I looked down at what she was wearing. She had black skinny jeans on, yet the fabric was soft. Her socks were white—I wasn't sure why I wanted to know what color socks she wore. My eyes traveled up to her sweatshirt. It was olive green, slightly oversized, and the sleeves were rolled up so her hands could peek out of them. Looking at it for some time, a small smirk appeared on my face.

"What?" she asked, gripping her sweatshirt with both hands and looking at it closely. "Is there a stain?"

I shook my head, looking up to her face now. "That's Jagger's," I said, recognizing the sweatshirt she was wearing. Her eyes met mine, embarrassed.

"My clothes haven't been washed yet since the accident. I didn't have anything to wear," she told me. I chuckled, taking her hands in mine.

"You look beautiful."

***

Harlow

His words never failed to make my heart beat faster. I knew I looked like a sack of potatoes in

Jagger's sweatshirt, but it was cold and my clothes were dirty. Jagger usually kept his stuff clean or just wore them more than once to work so he always had some spare shirts and pants. I had outfits for each day of the week, plus my work uniform. But since the accident, and therefore not being able to wash my clothes, I didn't have anything clean to wear besides the jeans and some underwear. Luckily, I owned more than just seven pairs of panties, bras, and socks.

"You should ask Jagger to go shop for new clothes. I know he's not using the money he's saving up but I think you need some more things to wear. Now that you know about the money, you should ask him about this one thing."

Hunter was right. I understood Jagger's intentions with that money. But I really was struggling most times with choosing what to wear. Hastings was fairly cold even in summer and one of the things I owned was a pair of shorts. I haven't worn them a lot, though.

"I might ask him," I said and smiled. Jagger wouldn't say no.

"Good. And as much as I appreciate Jagger letting you wear his sweatshirt, I want you to have one of mine instead. That's fucking corny, Jesus Christ," he mumbled and brushed his hand through his hair, shaking his head.

I laughed, my nose crinkling up in amusement. "A bit. But I'd love to have one of yours. Just to…keep you close."

He let out a laugh and then grinned. "Oh, good." This time, I was the one leaning forward to kiss him. I wasn't sure how we would ever make it in time to eat dinner with Jag and Bliss, but being five minutes or even ten late would be all right, I thought.

His tongue curled around mine as soon as I touched his and I couldn't help but let out a small moan. He pulled me closer, his arms around my waist tightly and the kiss deepening more and more. It felt good, noticing how passionate he was. His kiss was slow yet determined and I was sure that was all I ever wanted.

My hands made their way back into his hair, grabbing fistfuls and pulling at them slightly, knowing he liked the feeling of it. My heart was full, and even if I was the one being corny, I could feel our heartbeats' rhythm match.

His hands moved, making their way down to my behind. He cupped both of my butt cheeks and squeezed, making me moan. "God, your ass is perfect," he said into the kiss and I couldn't help but smile. Compliments he made about my body always surprised me, then excited me. I didn't do any sports and I was just lucky to have some good genes. Also, I didn't eat as much, yet I had some curves I was proud of.

"I think we're getting a bit carried away," I told him, not able to get away. He made it so hard to just stop making out or touching him.

He let out a low chuckle, then we both managed to get some distance between us. He looked at me with a cocky grin, then brushed my hair back from my cheeks, cupping my face into his hands. "What are you doing to me?" he said, almost whispering.

Frankly, if I had the answer to the same question for him, I would tell him.

CHAPTER TEN

Harlow

We made it to the diner and sat down at the booth Bliss reserved for us. The table was set for four and I noticed Bliss was not wearing her uniform. She sat down on the other side of the table, grinning widely and letting her eyes go from Hunter to me several times without ever saying a word. That made me laugh and I wrinkled my nose, tilting my head to the side.

"Why are you looking at us like that?" I asked.

"I have this gift of knowing when two people are in love," she simply said, making me slowly but surely realize what she was on about.

Hunter rolled his eyes, leaning back. "You also have the gift of being an annoying shit," he murmured, making me sigh and shake my head. "Hunter…"

"You two came in here smiling and holding hands like a married couple. First time I've seen him like that, and I think I like it." Bliss was still smiling brightly at us. I noticed Hunter's hand on my thigh, which had been lingering there since we sat down.

I pressed my lips into a thin line, trying not to turn red all over my face. I wasn't sure what to answer so I just kept looking down at his hand.

"Get used to it." Hunter's simple response was better than I had imagined. I looked up, not being able to hide a smile.

"Aw, man," Bliss said. "I was scared at first, knowing how he could get and seeing him treat you like shit. But I got high hopes now."

As much as I appreciated Bliss's words, I felt the tension rising in Hunter. I knew he didn't like talking about his anger issues. So, I did the only good thing and stepped in before something messy would happen.

"Hey, Bliss," I started, looking over at her. "I wanted to say I'm sorry for being rude and pretty much kicking you out."

Bliss laughed and waved her hand in refusal. "No need to feel bad, honey. You had every right to be mad and angry. Didn't take it personally."

Thankful for that, I nodded and gave her a smile, relaxing at the thought of her not being angry with me.

"Ah, and here comes the dirty one outta the bunch," Bliss said, looking over to my brother who was walking toward us, and she was now grinning again but this time there was something in her eyes I couldn't quite explain. Almost as if she had a dirty secret. And her calling him the dirty one was probably directed to his dirty clothes from working on cars, right?

Jagger walked up to our booth, giving Bliss a quick, warning glance and then smiling down at me. He bent his head, kissing the top of mine. "Hey, sweet girl. You feelin' okay?" he asked, sitting down next to Bliss, who now scooted over to sit opposite of Hunter. I nodded, returning his smile.

"I feel fine," I told him.

Jagger acknowledged my answer with a nod, then turned his gaze to look at Hunter. I held my breath, wanting to scream at those little voices in my head still telling me that Jagger hated the idea of Hunter and me together. I should've pushed those thoughts aside. I knew Jagger probably didn't like it, but he somehow accepted it.

"I got a call. It's done," Jagger said, taking off his cap and putting it next to him on the table. Hunter gave him a nod and that conversation was already finished. No more questions, no more talking.

"So, you guys wanna try our new burgers?" Bliss asked, giving each of us a questioning look. I nodded.

"Sounds good to me." The guys agreed and Bliss lifted her hand in the air, calling out to her co-worker and telling her to get the four of us those new burgers on the menu. We all ordered our drinks and when the waitress was gone again, Bliss started talking again.

***

Hunter

My sister's voice was too damn obtrusive. I loved her but hearing her go on and on about her day at work and how annoying some customers were wasn't really my passion. To distract me from that squeaky voice, I grabbed Low's hand in mine and pulled it into my lap, interlocking our fingers. I loved how small her hand was compared to mine, yet it fit right into it.

When Jagger told me that he got a call I held my breath for a second. It was an important call to let us know whether we had to go after one idiot tonight who thought it was a good idea to break into the cave and mess with Gunner personally. I didn't feel like working tonight. All I wanted to do was keep Harlow close and not let anybody ruin my night with her. I hadn't asked her yet if she'd want to come back to my place again tonight, but I was hoping she would say yes.

When we got the food, Harlow started eating immediately, almost as if she hadn't had any food in her system in weeks. She let go of my hand, using both of hers to grab the burger and take big bites, making sure one or two fries would get in that mouth too. It was amusing and kinda hot. She didn't mind people watching her eat or her getting sauce all over her cheeks. Of course, she wasn't eating like some kind of pig, all messy and dirty. But she enjoyed her food in the most adorable way possible.

"Jesus, you gonna stare at her some more or start eating too?" Jagger sounded amused yet annoyed.

"He's been bitten by the love bug a bit too hard,

I think," my sister explained, making me roll my eyes and grab my own burger now.

"She's just fascinating," I murmured before taking a bite, and out of the corner of my eyes, I saw a silly grin spread all over Harlow's face.

At least she was enjoying my embarrassment.

When did I turn into such a pussy-whipped softie?

After dinner, we kept on talking about some things, but I mostly listened to Bliss tell her stories about guys she met here and there. Some of the stories were amusing and Harlow listened to them with interest sparkling in her eyes. But something was slightly more amusing than watching Harlow listen to my sister's men-stories.

Jagger looked pissed. He rolled his eyes multiple times, shook his head or gripped his hair tightly. It was amusing at first because I thought he was just annoyed by her stories, but then I noticed some sort of jealousy as soon as another guy was mentioned by Bliss.

Shit. Were they fucking? I glanced between them, noticing for the first time how close Bliss sat to Jagger. Her voice came off mocking a lot of the time, and I wondered if she was just making him jealous.

Either way, and no matter if they were fucking, I was the last person allowed to get angry at them. I was with his sister too.

Though, I wasn't just fucking Harlow.

Not yet.

And even then, love would be involved in it and play a big fucking part too.

Chapter Eleven

Harlow

Living life was much easier knowing the people you loved the most loved you back no matter what. After everything that happened in that short amount of time, I finally felt peaceful. I had Hunter, who wasn't leaving my side, and any chance he got he spent his time with me. And there was Jagger, who still worked hard and made sure I was healthy and well. And then there was also Bliss, with whom I was spending more time. Of course, that only happened if Hunter was okay with letting me go out with his sister for some hours before kidnapping me back to his place as usual.

Watching Hunter's behavior change was incredibly astonishing. Not only was he much calmer with fewer outbursts, but the way he talked to others or reacted to stupid comments about him being 'pussy-whipped,' as Jagger liked to call it, was acceptable now. He learned to just let those comments slide and not make a big deal out of it.

There were days when Hunter couldn't keep it in, though. I didn't know what it was that triggered him, but he had gotten a message, and after reading it he threw his phone against the wall. Right after that, his fist landed on the spot on the wall his phone hit before. Blood ran down his forearm thanks to his then busted knuckles. I sat there on his couch, watching him pace in front of me and say some words I wished didn't exist. He pretty much damned the whole town and some guys I didn't quite catch the names of.

I waited for him to calm down, hoping I could keep my mouth shut and just be patient. Luckily, I was strong enough to keep in anything I wanted to say to help him relax. It took him about fifteen minutes to sit down next to me, not saying a word and letting me hug his side. He apologized, sighing deeply and kissing the top of my head. I told him it was okay and that I was proud of him for handling this situation that well. Sure, it was kinda stupid to tell him that, but in his mind, it helped reinforce his better behavior.

Another night we went over to my house, cooking dinner together and eating it with Jagger and Bliss. That was a weird evening. First, Hunter and Jagger discussed business, made a phone call all serious and tense, then came back laughing and took some beer out of the fridge to make a toast.

"Cheers to us," they said with a grin and Bliss and I just laughed and grabbed ourselves something to drink too.

After dinner, Jagger and Bliss suddenly disappeared outside, arguing loudly. We could only hear some muffled sounds on the inside, exchanging looks and making out our own scenarios in our heads. They came back inside, Bliss with a satisfied grin on her face and Jagger looked annoyed.

It was clear that they had a thing going on. Not sure why they even tried to hide it. I wouldn't mind them being a couple. If Jagger was happy, that was all that mattered. But the thing that kept them from telling us was Hunter. I could read Hunter all too well now and I knew when he disapproved of something or wasn't sure what to think of something. No matter if they were dating or just having sex it wasn't his business and he literally had no right to judge.

But what was his business was our sex life. Or how I liked to call it: our non-existing sex life. All right, I was exaggerating. After my first time giving him a blowjob, we, well, I started to experiment more. We were all over each other, not being able to get our hands off each other's bodies. Yet, we never managed to get to the sex part. I was sure it would be coming sooner or later, but two weeks was even too long of a stretch for me. And hell, I had no clue what it really was like. I was just excited to have my first time with Hunter. Knowing he knew what to do made me feel safe.

Hunter had told me many times that he didn't want to hurt me. He saw my greenish-yellow bruises around my upper body. "If I'm gonna have sex with you, I want to be able to touch you anywhere," he said. I wasn't hurting anymore, and I had told him that multiple times. But he didn't believe me.

Of course, I couldn't wait any longer. Everything else we did, the kissing, the blowjobs I gave him, and the orgasms he made me have, wasn't off-limits and felt great. I asked Bliss why Hunter wasn't making the next move.

"I think he just likes to fuck hard. All men do. They wanna take control over your body," was Bliss's response. I awkwardly laughed it off at first, but after asking Hunter about what Bliss had told me he agreed with his sister. Hearing Hunter approving only made me more excited and ready.

To make sure it was going to happen soon, I called the doctor to ask if I could go by and get checked because I wanted to start working out and I wasn't sure if I was allowed to yet. Of course, that was a lie, but telling them I wanted to make sure I could have sex without my boyfriend breaking my ribs again because he liked to fuck hard wasn't an option.

I told Hunter about the appointment and he quickly agreed to go with me. That was perfect, so he could hear Dr. Sullivan say that I was doing okay. Of course, Hunter didn't know about the lie I told the nurse. That would just make it awkward. Hunter knew I hated sports and workouts. The only walking I liked to do was at Frankie's, waiting tables, where I started working again a week ago.

So, here we were, me sitting on an examination table and Hunter on the seat next to it. He looked a little uneasy, almost worried. When I lifted a brow, he gave me a smile and sighed deeply.

"Just want you to be fit," he said. I rolled my eyes, wrinkling my nose.

"I told you before, Hunter. I feel fine and nothing's hurting anymore. You just don't believe me."

"Your body is still bruised, love."

"So, if the doc says my ribs are healed, will you still not touch me because of the bruises?" I asked. God, why was it so hard to make him fuck me?

He shrugged. "I don't wanna break you. That's all." I shook my head, murmuring something under my breath. He chuckled, which made me look back up at him only to see him grin like an idiot. "Is there something you want to tell me, sweetheart?" I shook my head once again, hoping he didn't hear what I said just then. "Harlow." He raised his eyebrows. "I heard you say something about sex." Great. So, he did hear something. I sighed this time, looking into his eyes. "Tell me," he pushed, leaning forward and propping his elbows on his knees.

"I just want to have sex," I told him. No need to try and fight him over this. He would get it out of me eventually, so I thought I'd just give up right then and there. The corners of Hunter's mouth went up, then his lips puckered. "You think I don't know that?" How dare he even say that? "So why won't you let me have it?"

What he said next should've been bleeped. Hunter had a dirty mind and even dirtier mouth and I was lucky Dr. Sullivan didn't come in and hear what Hunter said. "Because every time I fuck your sweet pussy with my tongue and fingers I feel how tight you are and the way you scream my name just from that makes me realize each damn time that the second my dick would push into that sweetness you

56

wouldn't be able to take it and I wouldn't be able to stop from pumping into you without mercy."

My mouth was dry, but my panties felt wet and hot. I kept staring at him, not able to say a word but imagining everything he just said. "And that's why. Just making sure you'll be able to handle me."

Whether or not he was trying to scare me or excite me, all I wanted to do was strip naked and fall all over him right in that doctor's office.

CHAPTER TWELVE

Hunter

Harlow was testing me. While Dr. Sullivan checked on her, her eyes wandered all over my body, pausing at where my cock was hiding underneath my jeans for too long most times. Her gaze was full of desire, that much I could tell. And even after telling her what I wanted to do with her, she didn't get scared away. Of course, I wanted that too, but I knew the way I could get during sex. I could go slow at first, just to make sure she'd adjust to the feeling of it, but as soon as it felt right and good for her, I wouldn't hold back.

I was amused by her attempt to tell me silently how ready she was for it. As a response, I simply smirked at her. That only frustrated her more, and I was sure the second we would get back to my trailer, she wouldn't hesitate to strip down her clothes and throw herself at me. But that would only happen if Dr. Sullivan told us that she was all healed up and fit again.

"So, my nurse told me you want to start doing some fitness," Sullivan said and smiled at Harlow. "I think that's a great idea. Just some running and fitness? Or are you a team player kinda girl?" he asked, and I raised both brows, giving Harlow a questioning look. Harlow didn't like any type of sports. She liked walking. But that's it.

Harlow suddenly tensed up and pressed her lips into a thin line. She looked at me, then turned slightly red on her cheeks and turned her gaze back to Sullivan. "I just..." she started. I was waiting for a response, but before she continued, I realized why we were here in the first place. I started to grin again, knowing she needed an excuse to come here and get checked. "Just some running," she told Sullivan and I couldn't help but chuckle.

"That's awesome. I can assure you that everything is fine. As long as you're not hurting, you should be good to go on some runs. Your lungs have regained some strength. The bruises are healing up well, so I don't see a reason why running wouldn't be a good idea. Maybe it will even help your lungs to get back to their normal state."

Harlow nodded, then gave me a quick look, not embarrassed anymore but to let me know that she knew I had figured her plan out. Her eyes said, "I told you I was all better." I shrugged, still amused by the whole situation.

"Now, I'll let you two go before I start feeling left out of your silent conversation." Sullivan got up from his chair and let out a soft chuckle, shaking his head. "Take good care of her, son."

I nodded, smiling at Harlow, who was now

getting up from the table. "I will," I told him, standing up from my chair and reaching for Harlow's hand. "The best part is that she has no clue how wrapped up she has me around her little finger."

***

Harlow

He knew. He knew I lied to the nurse and he caught me red-handed when Dr. Sullivan blurted it out. At first, I was embarrassed, but then I reminded myself that it probably was best if he just knew how much I wanted it. He wouldn't believe me when I told him that I wasn't hurting, and I had to find some excuse to go to the doctor.

But no matter how it all went down, I was happy that he didn't get angry but just laughed it off. Though, he mocked me on the drive back to his trailer, telling me how funny it was when I turned all red in my face. He also said it was cute the way I planned it all just because I wanted finally to go further.

The second we arrived at the trailer park, Hunter got out of the car and walked over to open my car door. I took his hand and stepped out, only to be pulled into his arms. He cupped my face with both his hands, tilting his head down to kiss my lips softly.

I grabbed both his shoulders to steady me. Every kiss he gave me still weakened my knees no matter how many times we made out. His tongue brushed over my lips, making me open up my mouth more to touch my tongue to his. I loved the way he explored and took his time just kissing me. The kiss got deeper, and I let out a small moan, letting him know I was getting frustrated. I was pressing my hips against him and trying to get closer than ever. I felt his body tensing and his kiss grew more passionate.

Suddenly, his hands moved down to cup my bottom, lifting me so I wrapped my legs around his hips, not breaking the kiss once. Before walking up to the trailer, he closed the car door by kicking it with his foot. He wasn't taking his hands off me and I liked it. When we got to the door, he pushed me against it and I could tell he was getting hard. Good. Just what I wanted. To open the door, Hunter let me down, breaking the kiss for a short amount of time just to take out his keys and open it. When we got inside, he locked the door and looked at me, standing in the middle of his living room.

"I need you naked and in my bed," he told me, nodding to the bedroom. I gave him a smile, then quickly took off my sweatshirt. He watched me as I lifted off the shirt—I was wearing nothing underneath—and threw it onto the couch, not really bothered that it fell to the ground. Next were my pants, and the second I pushed them down my legs, Hunter took off his sweater and shirt all at once.

He was getting impatient and something about that amused me. At first, I was the one pushing him to have sex, now he was looking more prepared than ever, licking his lips while letting his eyes wander all over my panty-covered body.

CHAPTER THIRTEEN

Hunter

She watched me undress, still standing there in her pretty little panties, her chest rising and falling with each deep breath she took. She looked relaxed. Normally, girls who were about to have their first time were nervous, but not Harlow. Sweet Harlow was ready and willing. I was the one keeping my distance and stopping myself from going further than what we did usually, but now I wasn't sure I'd be able to stop touching her after feeling myself inside of her. My cock was already hard, just waiting to be squeezed by her.

As I took a few steps toward her, Harlow stepped back, slowly making her way to the open bedroom. A smirk appeared on my face and I couldn't help a shake of my head.

"You really want this, huh?" I said, following her to the bed. She simply nodded. When the back of her knees met the bed, she came to a halt and I could finally wrap my arms around her waist. Her breasts pressed against my chest and the fabric of her panties and my shorts rubbed against each other. I wished there was nothing between us. Those two layers were too many. With my thumbs, I hooked her panties on the sides and pushed them down. When they were down to the middle of her thighs, Harlow sat back onto the bed, then leaned back on her elbows and lifted her legs to let me take those panties off fully.

I threw them behind me, not caring where they landed, and finally got to appreciate her beautiful body in full view. My eyes were all over her, from her perfect breasts to her stomach, down to her shaved pussy and her legs. Her skin was soft.

Harlow kept looking at me, amusement dancing in her eyes. "Are you enjoying the view?" she asked, letting me know she was comfortable and enjoying me staring at her. Her growing confidence was amazing. Not that I ever thought she wasn't confident but seeing her evolve right in front of my eyes was something I would remember forever. I didn't have many people opening up to me the way she did, and that was why I believed she was the right girl for me. She trusted me. Even after everything I had told her, she stuck to me and didn't judge or run away.

"Please, don't make me wait any longer, Hunter." Her soft voice was almost pleading, and I realized I was staring at her a little too long. I took a mental picture of her like that, then stepped up to the bed and leaned over her, holding myself up with one hand next to her head.

"Just making sure this is all real and not just in

my head," I whispered before kissing her. I could feel a smile tugging on her lips, then her hands reached up to run through my hair. As usual, that sent some major jolts right down to my dick. She knew I liked the way she played with my hair and the fact that she was teasing me with it while lifting her hips to meet mine was making it all even more exciting. I pressed her hips back down with mine, letting her feel my hardness and receiving a small moan in return. That was it.

***

Harlow

As much as I was trying to keep my cool on the outside, on the inside I was screaming and wishing he would just take off his shorts. I felt the heat between my legs and now, with just the fabric of his shorts between us, I was getting closer and closer to what I'd wanted for weeks. If felt good, him rubbing his length against me. His hips moved slowly but he touched all the right spots down there.

I didn't want to let go of his hair, yet I needed his shorts to be gone. Moving my hands downward, I hooked my fingers inside the waistband and pushed them down. Luckily, Hunter helped me take them off him and threw them to the side. I broke the kiss, looking into his eyes before I gazed down to see his length lay there on my lower stomach. The familiar red tip of his cock told me he was ready and the small dot of precum, which I learned about the very first time I gave him a blowjob, meant that

I had turned him on more than just a little. I reached down, wrapping my hand around the base and stroking him up to the tip, where I ran my thumb over the tip, sweeping away the small drop of precum.

"Fuck," he murmured, lowering his head to kiss my neck. I moved my hand up and down his cock, now looking at his face. He had lifted his head again to look down at my hand pumping him, and a deep crease appeared between his brows.

"What's wrong?" I asked, stopping my hand and touching my other one to his cheek. He gave me a little grin, shaking his head.

"Just amazes me how I can't get enough of you." He sighed, but not in a bad way. "You're all I want, love, and I swear I will make this so fucking good for you."

I never doubted that. But hearing him say it while looking me in the eyes with such honesty just melted my heart. I smiled at him, kissing him softly and then looking back up at him. "I love you, Hunter. You're all I want too."

Chapter Fourteen

Hunter

The smell of her arousal was all around us and I couldn't think straight, kissing my way down to her breasts. I cupped one of them in my hand, squeezing her nipple between my finger and thumb. A moan escaped her and with one glance up to her face, I covered the other nipple with my mouth, my tongue flicking the hard nub. The way she moved her hips against me let me know she needed me to stop teasing her, but I wasn't stopping there. I wanted to taste her once more before burying myself inside of her. I'd tasted her before, making her come on my tongue, hearing her scream out my name and begging me to keep going.

I glanced up at her again, keeping her nipple in my mouth and tugging on it slightly.

"Hunter, please," she begged, her eyes now meeting mine. At first, I didn't like her begging for it, not wanting to hurt her. But now, hearing and watching her get all worked up like that made me even harder.

"Be patient, love," I said mockingly, getting an eye roll from her.

"Are you kidding me?" she said under her breath. I chuckled, nibbling at her other nipple and moving one hand down to her wetness. The second I ran my fingers through her center, another moan escaped her. "Please, Hunter." She lifted her hips again. I raised my head to look down at her, my finger now circling her clit.

"You gonna let me taste you first?" I asked, knowing that she loved the way I could make her feel with my tongue. Her eyes were full of desire and a shiver came over her. A small nod from her and I was already on my way down to that sweetness I lusted over every fucking time she was naked.

I kissed my way down to her stomach slowly. She buckled underneath me, restless, and I inhaled that sweet scent. Reaching the spot I dreamed about so often was my goal, but of course, I couldn't just give her what she wanted without teasing her a little more. Pushing her legs apart even further, I lowered my head to kiss the insides of her thighs, holding them open. Her legs were shaking slightly and I knew she was just waiting for me to lick and kiss her pussy. The first stroke of my tongue came shortly after some more kisses along her thighs. I decided not to make her wait longer. Her moans told me she was probably not gonna be able to be patient any longer. The way she pulled my hair confirmed my theory.

My tongue flicked at her entrance, then circled

her swollen clit. I knew exactly what I was doing to her and I liked being in control of her body. Harlow bucked her hips, moaning my name. I put one hand on her stomach, pressing her down to make her stop moving and so I could keep on tasting her.

"Hunter!" she screamed, grabbing onto my hair even tighter and I knew she was close. Whenever we did this before, I couldn't stop until she came back down from her orgasm and I wasn't going to stop now, either.

***

Harlow

He was incredible. I knew every time he made me come that it was the best feeling ever. But I also knew that this time would be different. I wanted to go a step further. Feel him inside me. After that orgasm, I kept my eyes closed and tried to breathe normally again. I felt Hunter giving me some soft kisses on my stomach, then on each breast. I opened my eyes again, looking straight into his and smiling.

"You okay?" he asked in a whisper, carrying a smug grin on his face.

"Yes," I told him and kissed his lips. His tongue came out to touch mine and I could taste myself on him. He broke the kiss after a while, reaching for his bedside table. I watched as he pulled out a condom, smiling down at me.

"I'm really trying to be good, sweetheart." I pressed my lips together, trying to figure out why he always said that. But then Bliss's words came into mind. She said men liked to have control over women. I could tell with Hunter and we were about to have our first time. But I couldn't imagine why he was warning me so much.

"I'm not scared. I want this. And I want to feel you inside of me." I needed him to know. He wasn't going to break me and I sure as hell wasn't going to keep him from showing me just how good sex could be. "Just be yourself. Don't change just because you think you could hurt me. I can handle it. And you," I told him. A chuckle escaped him, and he shook his head for a second.

"You're fucking incredible."

Hunter pushed himself up on his knees to put on the condom. I watched as he opened the small package, threw it to the ground, and pulled the condom over his hard length. He looked almost pained doing it, as if the condom was hurting. But then, I could imagine it being a little uncomfortable. I let my eyes wander up to his stomach, then his chest and wide shoulders. The sight of him like that was incredibly hot. Biting my bottom lip, I reached up to touch his not too defined muscles. I loved the way he looked. He had just the right amount of muscles and he wasn't like one of those extremely trained, body builder-looking guys. He was just perfect.

"Keep eye-fucking me like that and I won't be able to hold back, sweetheart." His voice was deep but amused and I couldn't help but smile. I looked into his eyes, reaching up my hand to pull him down by putting my hand on his neck.

"Maybe that's what I want," I teased, kissing his

lips. A growl came from his chest and I could feel his tip at my entrance. Yes, just where I wanted it.

CHAPTER FIFTEEN

Hunter

I was trying really fucking hard not to just push into her and make her scream from pain. I was more than ready though, and Harlow seemed to be a little too comfortable with the whole situation. I've known her for a while now and at first, I always thought she would be one of those wallflowers, not even thinking about sex or anything that came close to that, but she proved me wrong some days ago by asking me if she could explore my body the way I explored hers. Just that almost sent me over the edge. Turned out sweet Harlow was wild.

Not complaining about that. Ever.

I broke the kiss, adjusting myself over her and touching the tip of my cock to her entrance. It felt warm and wet, just how I wanted her.

"You trust me?" I asked. I knew she did, but I needed to hear it from her. She gave me a nod and a sweet smile.

"Always, Hunter."

With a slow push, I felt her heat squeezing me, and even if I wanted to, I don't think I could've stopped. I watched her beautiful face as I filled her with my hardness and prayed to God that I wasn't hurting her. It felt too damn good. She gave me a smile after a deep crease appeared on her forehead.

"I'm okay," she whispered, and I bent down to kiss her lips, not moving when I felt something stopping me from going deeper. I was fully inside her, trying not to move back and slam into her with force. I knew she said she was all right, but I didn't want to scare her by the way I liked to fuck. She had to be prepared for that.

"Want me to move?" I asked her, already knowing the answer and chuckling when she rolled her eyes at me.

"Please, Hunter. It feels amazing." I couldn't help but smirk, then moved back slowly, only to push back inside of her, getting the first moan out of her. I kept doing just that, watching her closely to figure out how much she could handle. Her right hand gripped my arm, her left touched my waist. I knew she was trying to control my movements, but she still looked pretty relaxed. Her lips were slightly apart, and her breathing hitched now and then. Her eyes stayed on mine the whole time and I knew at that moment that no one else could ever take her place.

When I knew she was feeling okay, I bent down to kiss her again, then started to move faster and with more force. Our tongues met and moans escaped her mouth. I rested my right elbow next to her head, cupping the top of her head with my hand

and gripping some hair in my fist. I started to move even faster, keeping control over her. My other hand made its way down to her hips, pushing her down slightly so she would stop meeting my thrusts. Even if it helped me get deeper inside of her, I wanted to have all the control. Knowing from her movements that she needed more, I started to pump into her harder, making her break the kiss again and scream my name.

"You're so fucking tight, love," I told her while trying to catch my breath. Not just being inside her, but also the sight of her pleasured face and those tits bouncing up and down made me all sorts of worked up. "Fuck, you have no idea how fucking amazing you feel. So wet too."

My name fell from her lips again and again. The more she did that, the harder and faster I moved inside her. I felt my cock tighten, ready to let go and fill her. Sounded weird, but I wanted to mark her. Make sure she knew how good it felt for me to come inside of her. Of course, the condom was still between us, but we could work our way around that. Maybe someday she'd be ready to take the pill. Feeling her around my cock, squeezing me just right, that's what I wanted.

***

Harlow

It burned. But the burning was better than I ever imagined. It felt good and right. And even if it was my first time, I wanted Hunter to just be himself and not trying to make sure I wasn't hurting. I wasn't. I just had to get used to it.

The way he stretched me and moved his hips with quick thrusts excited me. Not only that but the hair he gripped and pulled tight on my head made the whole thing even better. He was taking control, just like Bliss said. But I liked it. I felt safe and protected in his arms and the gentle yet deep kisses he gave me let me know that he was still being gentle with me.

I could tell Hunter was close. The way he squeezed his eyes shut multiple times and stopping for some seconds to adjust again and catch his breath told me that he was trying to hold back something. I watched as he covered my nipple with his mouth while still pumping into me with hard thrusts. His tongue ran over the hard nub, then he bit down on it, making me squeal and laugh.

"Hunter." He looked up, licking over it once more and then kissing my lips.

"You okay?" he asked, looking back into my eyes with concern.

"Yes. It feels perfect," I told him. A smile appeared on his lips and he started to move faster again.

"I swear, this pussy is gonna send me straight to heaven," he murmured and now I smiled at his dirty words.

Suddenly, I felt something building up down in my belly, making me close my eyes and throw my head back and to the side. "Oh, Hunter," I moaned, lifting my hips to meet his thrusts. Hunter's hand came up around my neck, squeezing gently and letting out a growl.

"Fuck, love, let me feel you come on my dick," he said in a low, hoarse voice. I let out another moan, surprised by the feeling overcoming me. I had read many times that a woman is most likely not going to come from her first time. I had my mind set on it. Until now. I knew it was coming. Literally.

"Hunter!" I screamed as I felt him move harder. He wasn't stopping and I was starting to believe that what we had was magical.

"Let go, sweetheart. Let me feel that tight pussy squeezing me." That was it. The way he pushed me with his words made the whole thing even better. Warmth came over me, making me want to press my thighs together and scream as loud as I could.

"Oh, God! Hunter, please." I wasn't sure what I was begging for, but the feeling stuck, making me lightheaded. I gripped both his arms with my hands, holding him tight, and then feeling his cock pulsate inside of me.

"Fuck!" he growled, now moving just a little while he came. "So fucking tight.".

I opened my eyes to watch him, wanting to keep that image in my head forever. His head was low, eyes closed, and every single muscle in his body was tensed. When I finally was able to move again, I cupped his face with both my hands and pulled him down to kiss him.

"You're mine," he mumbled, making me smile. Nodding, I ran my hands through his hair.

"Forever," I told him.

CHAPTER SIXTEEN

Hunter

We spent the rest of the night in my bed, not taking our hands off each other. I had asked Harlow one too many times how she was feeling, not wanting her to hurt after our first time. I wasn't really holding back, though she asked for me to go harder. She told me that she was fine, feeling some sort of tingling down there. That was all right for now. She wasn't walking yet, so I had to wait until she got up and realized that the tingling sensation she felt was from being sore.

I couldn't stop running my hands over her body and kissing her, telling her I loved her multiple times. She always returned my words with a sweet and pleased smile. *Lucky me*, I thought. I was the one taking care of her and making sure she was feeling good. I was the one now to protect her. But then I remembered something Jagger said some years ago. About Dean not treating her and him right. He told me that Dean started hitting him when he was still a toddler, then when Harlow was old enough to understand what Dean was doing, he did it to her too. But not only that. The disgusting things their father did to her was one good fucking reason to just blow his brains out. I never really asked Jagger for more details, but what he said that time was enough for me to understand.

"What's wrong?" Harlow asked, turning her head to look up at me but keeping it on my chest. Her arm was wrapped around my waist, her legs intertwined with mine. Since our first time, I only left the bed once to get rid of the condom and get some water for Low. Since then, we stayed in bed, wrapped up under the cover, just how I liked it.

"Hm?" I looked at her, brushing back some hair and tugging it behind her ear.

"You're tense," she whispered, seemingly worried. I shook my head, sighing and running my other hand through my hair.

"I just remembered something. But I don't wanna make you sad or dig too deep."

"What is it?" She pushed herself up, sitting up and pulling the covers up to cover her bare body. The deep crease between her brows was back and I wondered why I was the one causing that every time. I sighed, pushing myself up, too and leaning back against the wall behind me.

"I really don't mean to open up an old wound, sweetheart. I know you're all better now."

Harlow watched me closely, then a small smile crossed her face and her eyes fell to look at her own hands.

"But?" she asked. I wasn't sure she knew what I

was talking about. I guess she was making sure herself.

"But I just want you to know that I'm here from now on and won't let anything happen to you. Ever. And if you want to talk to me about it, or anything, I will listen."

***

Harlow

I knew what he was talking about. I just wasn't sure who had told him about it. But then, only Jagger knew about my past. I never told anyone about my childhood. It didn't feel necessary to tell anyone. Besides, I didn't want to bother anyone with my worries. Knowing Hunter wanted me to talk about it now was a bit weird. We just had our first time, and it was beautiful. But talking about what Dean did to me when I was only four years old was kinda hard. I knew I could trust Hunter. But it still didn't feel right to talk about it. With anyone.

I took a deep breath, my gaze back on his eyes. "I don't wanna talk about it." It came out a bit harsh. But I hoped Hunter would understand. He reached up to cup my cheek, giving me a soft smile.

"And that's okay. Just know that you'll never bother me. No matter what. If there's something you wanna tell me, I'll listen."

I gave him a quick nod, laying back down to cuddle up to him. I buried my face into his neck and closing my eyes. "I know that. And I'll forever be thankful."

Hours passed and neither of us seemed to care much about getting up and doing something with the remaining evening ahead of us. It felt nice just lying there with him, but I had to get back home. I had work in the morning and as usual, I had to get up early.

"Hunter," I said, looking up at him and turning my head. His eyes were closed, but I knew he wasn't sleeping. "Hunter, I need to go home. Jagger will be back from work soon."

A low growl escaped him, and I couldn't help but laugh at the way he wrinkled his nose. "Already?" he asked, now opening his eyes to look at me.

I nodded, running my hand through his hair and kissing his cheek softly. "I promised him dinner. And you know how tired he is after work."

"Will you come back here after you have dinner?" he asked, and I thought about it for a second. God, why was he so adorable without even trying?

"I have work tomorrow." I wanted to sound serious to let him know that I couldn't spend the night with him, or we wouldn't sleep. That much I knew about us. Every time I spent the night, we either talked all night long or we just couldn't stop our hands and mouths from exploring each other.

"I can drive you. And then, when you get off work tomorrow night, I can pick you up and we'll come back here again."

I let out a small laugh, shaking my head. "You really think that's a good idea?" He shrugged.

"Probably not. But you know exactly how much

I hate it when you have to walk to work or back home all on your own." I did know that, but I also told him more than once that I was old enough to do it on my own.

"Are we really having that conversation again?" I asked, raising an eyebrow.

"No. But let me at least drive you home."

Agreeing with that, we both got up and got dressed, finding our clothes all over the floor. When we stepped out of his trailer, Hunter grabbed my hand and pulled me behind him, looking over to a black SUV. Before even questioning who it was, the car door opened and a man with a familiar face stepped out of the car.

"The fuck is that?" Hunter whispered, his other hand gripping something at the back of his jeans. His gun was tucked in there and I had to get used to him and Jagger carrying one around every day. I wasn't scared of guns but I sure as hell wasn't a fan.

"That's the man who questioned us about Dean at the police station in Grand Island. Tripp Bennett, I think," I told Hunter in a low voice, not wanting Bennett to hear for some reason. Hunter's hand loosened on the gun and my hand.

"No need to cause a scene here, Mr. Kane," Bennett said, walking toward us and stopping in front of the gate of Hunter's trailer. Bennett turned to look at me and a smile appeared on his face. "Miss Curtis, it's good to see you again. Glad I found you. Your brother told me you were here, just wasn't sure where to knock."

"Is Jagger okay?" I asked, hoping there was nothing wrong.

"Yes, your brother is all right. I talked to him for a second before coming here. I just wanted to check in on you." He took a glance at Hunter, then let his eyes wander up and down his body. I was so confused.

"I'm sorry, Mr. Bennett. But why?" I wondered if he knew about Jagger and Hunter working for Gunner. But how would he know? He looked back at me with a smirk on his face.

"Because I investigated your case with your father playing a huge role in it, and I wondered if you told me the whole truth or just sugarcoated it so Dean would get away with it."

"Does Jagger know that you're here because of Dean?" Hunter asked, seemingly annoyed and ready to burst. Shit, this wasn't going to end well. I touched my hands to Hunter's forearm, trying to calm him down. Bennett rolled his eyes at Hunter, then looked back at me.

"I'm trying to help you guys out, not going against you. Jagger knows. And he's waiting at home for us." He then nodded toward his car, walking back to it and opening the passenger seat.

Hunter raised an eyebrow, shaking his head. "She'll drive with me."

Bennett copied Hunter's facial expression, then closed the door again. "Right. See you there." He got into his car and drove off, making me question everything that just went down in the last five minutes.

Hunter was still tense, his fists tight at his sides. "Who the fuck does he think he is?" he muttered, shaking his head again. I looked up at him, sighing and kissing his lips softly.

"It's okay. We'll talk and then he'll be gone. I bet Jagger wouldn't have let him come here if something was wrong."

He nodded, then started walking toward his car, opening the gate. "Still a fucking piece of shit." That made me laugh a little, kinda agreeing with him this time. Tripp Bennett seemed much nicer back in Grand Island. He was just being cocky and pretty arrogant.

CHAPTER SEVENTEEN

Hunter

We arrived at Harlow's house, parking my car behind Jagger's. I glanced over to the other side of the road where Bennett got out of his SUV and started walking over to the house. He had a smug grin on his face, letting me know that he was aware of the way he pissed me off. Jagger had told me about an investigator helping with Dean's case, but I thought that time in Grand Island was the only time he would be helping. And I also didn't know that he was a total piece of shit, eye fucking my girl right in front of me.

"Stop scowling at him like that, Hunter." Harlow's voice sounded almost as amused as Bennett's face looked, and I raised an eyebrow, turning my head to look at her.

"You okay with him acting like he's the king of these streets?" I asked.

"You aren't, either," she told me matter-of-factly. "Now, come on. The sooner we get in there and talk, the sooner he'll leave." She got out of the car, leaving me in there alone, wondering when sweet Harlow shot back answers like that. I couldn't help but chuckle, knowing that my girl was strong and smart. She wasn't afraid of making me mad anymore. She just spoke her mind. And I liked it that way.

When I pulled all my shit together, I got out and walked up to the house, reaching for Harlow's hand when we got to the door. I just needed Bennett to know that she was mine. I made it clear back at my place, though I wanted him to remember it as much as possible.

When Harlow opened the door and called out for her brother, Bennett leaned in to whisper in my ear. "Loosen up some, boy." He then patted my shoulder a little too hard, which made his words come over just as mocking as he was before. Dipshit. He was acting like he wasn't just flirting with Harlow. But fuck, maybe I was just letting him mess with me a little too much.

I shook my head, following Harlow inside and then walking straight over to the fridge to get me a beer. Jagger appeared next to me, grabbing a can himself. "My phone's dead. So I sent him to come and get you guys."

I turned to him, lifting a brow and taking a long sip. "Ever heard of chargers?" I asked, annoyed.

Jagger shrugged, then walked back to the living room where he sat down in the recliner. Bennett was sitting on the couch, leaning back and propping one foot up on his knee.

"Would you like something to drink?" Harlow

asked him, walking over to where I was still standing in the doorway between the kitchen and living room.

"Water's just fine, thank you." She nodded, passing me and opening a cabinet to get a glass out. I turned with one last glance at Bennett, then stood behind Harlow at the sink.

"You sure we can trust him?" I asked, lowering my head so I could whisper.

"Yes. He's just helping, Hunter." She turned with a full glass of water in her hand, looking up at me with honesty-filled eyes. "Jagger wouldn't have let him in otherwise." Good point. Besides, we were two against one if Bennett decided to pull a gun. We had multiple hidden around the house, one just underneath his ass where he sat. But he didn't need to know that. He was still some sort of cop, right?

I studied her face for a while, wishing I could just take her to bed and do what we did some hours ago all over again. This time, without any form of being gentle. Although…

"Are you sore?" I asked, changing the subject and running my fingers through her long locks. A smile appeared on her face and her cheeks turned red.

"No," she whispered. "Maybe a little," she then added, not being able to hide it.

"Good," I said, lowering my head to kiss her lips softly. She immediately moved her lips against mine, reaching up her free hand to grab my arm. She was steadying herself, making sure she wouldn't drop the glass in her other hand. That's what I wanted to do rather than sit there and listen to Bennett talk. Just as I ran my tongue along her bottom lip, Jagger's voice interrupted what I was about to do next.

"Low, come on." She pushed against my chest, giving me a shy smile.

"Later", she told me, getting all my hopes up.

***

Harlow

I was feeling all hot and tingly inside because of Hunter's kiss back in the kitchen. It was just a simple kiss, yet it made me feel all types of ways and ready to go back to bed. I knew he was thinking the same. But we weren't alone, and I didn't want to make them feel uncomfortable. I sat down on the couch where Bennett was sitting and couldn't help a small grin when Hunter positioned himself right next to me, acting as some type of barrier between Bennett and me. I wasn't complaining, and just to let Hunter know that I was all his, I grabbed his hand and pulled it onto my lap.

"You're probably wondering why I'm here," Bennett started, looking at me and then Jagger. "After you left Grand Island, we had to let Dean go since you bailed him out. We couldn't let him leave unsupervised, though, since he was still a danger to other drivers on the road and people in general. So, we followed him around for a while, making sure he wouldn't start some shit along the way. He stopped at a motel, just sitting in his car and smoking. We told him before letting him go that if he got caught in an act of crime or riot of some sort, we would take him back to the PD and not call his kids to bail him out again. We couldn't just keep watching him all night long, so we went back, leaving him alone. We were lucky not to hear from him for some weeks until there was a report on some stolen and broken-in vehicles. We found three of the cars, but one wasn't found. That's when we got a call from the Hastings police department. The silver Subaru Legacy which was reported missing was seen around Hastings, but since we were aware of Dean sitting in it, we wanted to get at it slowly, not to cause any more trouble. He's not aware of us following him around. We just noticed some patterns. Now, I'm not trying to scare you." Bennett looked at me, his expression was serious. "He's following you around, watching you go to work and back home. He was also seen at the trailer park, just sitting in his car and waiting until Hunter's car pulled back out on the road."

"Motherfucker," Hunter growled, looking over at Jagger. "The fuck are you so calm about this?" he said, shaking his head.

Jagger sighed, rubbing his stubbled jaw. "Because it's Dean. The only way we could get rid of him is by getting him off this world."

"I wasn't talking about getting rid of him. What if he has a gun with him, huh? He's been following her around, for fuck's sake!" I gripped Hunter's hand tighter, turning to look at him.

"Nothing happened yet, Hunter."

He let out a harsh laugh, taking his hand from mine and standing up. "Is he out there now?" he asked, walking over to the window.

"No, he's not. My partner said he hasn't left his car yet and he's just sitting in an empty parking lot of a gas station. You really think I would've come here, showing myself to him?" Bennett asked, amused. God, this wasn't going to end well at all.

"Hunter, please sit back down," I said slowly, hoping he would listen.

"That bastard is creeping on you, Goddammit!" I sighed, trying to keep calm.

"I'm aware of that now, Hunter. But that's why Mr. Bennett is here. Please, sit back down."

It took Hunter several minutes to pace up and down the living room before sitting back down. I caressed his back and wrapped my other hand around his arm.

"Now, I get the frustration. We're trying to do our best here. Dean hasn't left his car in some days. Not sure how he's surviving but we've seen him eat some sandwiches in the past few days and he emptied some bucket multiple times."

A simultaneous, disgusted sound came out of us at the realization of what Dean was dumping out of his car. What a sad, sad man.

"So you guys are just letting him sit in there?" Jagger asked.

Bennett looked over at him, nodding. "We gotta be careful. We don't know if he's got guns with him. Not taking any risks. For now, I need you to be careful and know that I'm around to make sure Dean won't cross any lines."

Chapter Eighteen

Harlow

I could feel the tension in the room. Not only was Dean in town, but I could tell Hunter wasn't going to let that slip easily. No matter how calm he acted right now, I knew Dean and Bennett being around would have consequences. It bothered him that there was someone else protecting me from my father, but he just had to get along with that thought.

Bennett was still in our living room, sipping on his water and talking about all the possible reasons why Dean was in town. The fact that he had even found out where we lived was scary. I knew Dean wasn't just here to watch us, and since he didn't leave that stolen car and did his business in a bucket, he couldn't be safe to be around.

I patted Hunter's knee, giving him a small smile and hoping he would realize that even I had to keep calm. As much as I loved him, I needed him to step back a little and let the professionals do the work.

Sure, Jagger and Hunter were hitmen. They could easily go after Dean. But now that the police were informed, they couldn't just make Dean disappear. It would be a little too suspicious.

"What if the police tried to show themselves to Dean and let him know they're around?" I asked, wanting to help the situation. Bennett turned to look at me, shaking his head and lifting the corner of his mouth slightly.

"Gonna be honest with you here, Harlow," he said, putting his glass down. "Your father knows his way around the cops. He's a manipulator—"

Jagger's chuckle interrupted Bennett. "Nothing new," he muttered, taking another sip of his beer. "And in that case, we need to catch him off guard. See what he's up to and get to him when he least expects it. I know it's scary knowing he's around, but right now, we have no reason to arrest him."

Hunter let out a harsh laugh this time and we all glanced over to him. "He's fucking stalking her. Isn't that enough reason to arrest him?" he asked. He had a point. Stalking was a crime and should be taken seriously. Bennett shook his head. "He's keeping some distance for now. And the longer we try to just watch him, the more time we get to prepare for anything he could do."

My head was full. I didn't want to think about anything Dean would wanna do. He was an alcoholic. Drugs weren't rare in his system. I looked over at my brother who was watching me closely. I smiled at him, letting him know I was okay. I didn't need him to worry. We were all okay for now and that's what mattered.

"What about work?" Jagger then asked and turned to look at Bennett. "Is it safe for me to go to work?" Bennett shrugged.

"What do you do?" he asked, the question sounding a bit empty. Almost as if he already knew the answer.

"Mechanic," was Jagger's simple response. Bennett raised a brow, then looked over at Hunter.

"And what do you do?" I looked up at Hunter, pressing my lips into a thin line. I hope he had a good lie prepared for this situation because telling an investigator that you killed people for a living was the wrong answer.

We were waiting for an answer, but Hunter didn't seem to have one. I glanced over at Jagger, hoping he would help him out. Luckily, Hunter then answered and relief washed over me.

"I cook. At Frankie's Diner." Bennett nodded, Jagger gave him a confused look, and I tried not to grin like a fool because even if that wasn't true, I knew he meant it as an answer to my offer back then when I had asked him to work for Frankie.

***

Hunter

I just accepted Harlow's offer to work at Frankie's because of that piece of shit next to us. I didn't want to work. Hell, I wasn't even sure if Frankie still needed someone to help out in the kitchen. But the way Harlow beamed at me when I said it told me that the job was still open. Great.

91

"I wouldn't mind you guys working and keep on living, but I'm just a bit worried about her." Bennett nodded toward Harlow, and for the first time, I agreed with him. "She shouldn't be working late shifts or walking home alone," he said. "As long as one of you is always around her, it'll be fine. I know you got enough shit to handle but maybe try to stay in a bit more until Dean makes the next move."

"What if we just carry guns? If he tries something, we can defend ourselves," Jagger said. What was he trying to do? Jesus, Jagger.

"I know Hastings isn't a safe city, but carrying guns just makes it more difficult if Dean acts up and you pull one on him. Cops could arrest you just the same." Bennett had a point. He watched Jagger for a while, then turned his head to look at me. "Let me be clear here. I know you two are carrying. But it's your house," he said, looking back at Jagger. "And keeping guns in your own home isn't a crime. But going outside and even thinking about using them could get you in some deep shit."

"What makes you think we're carrying?" Jagger asked with his eyebrow shot up. He then lifted his shirt, revealing that he didn't have a gun tucked into his pants.

Bennett let out a small chuckle, shaking his head and leaning back. "And as soon as I'm out that door, a gun will be tucked in there."

Jagger leaned back as well. "What makes you think I got guns laying around the house?" he asked, almost challenging.

Bennett tilted his head to the side and a smug

grin appeared on his face. "You really think I can't feel that gun underneath the cushion?" I gave Jagger an annoyed look. Fucking touché, idiot.

I growled, running my hand over my face. "Can you just leave? We got this. She won't leave the house without one of us and you'll keep us updated on Dean, deal?" I said, getting up and needing to stretch my legs and relax again before I kicked him out myself. I'd seen enough of him for today.

Harlow's hand reached up to touch mine, giving me a serious look. "Be nice," she whispered as if Bennett wouldn't hear.

He then chuckled, standing up and nodding toward Jagger. "I got your number in case I got news." He turned to look at Harlow, giving her a smile now. "You keep these two down to earth, yeah? They seem to have more love for you than themselves."

Harlow nodded slowly, smiling back at him. "Thank you. For helping out, I mean," she told him. Right, that was enough of him staring at her. I walked him over to the door and opened it to send him on his way.

Bennett had other plans, though. He stopped and turned to me. His hand once again landed on my shoulder, gripping it a little too tightly for my liking. "Listen, man. I'm here to help. Jagger sees it and your girl sees it too. Now stop giving me those looks. She's all yours." With one last pat on my shoulder, he left.

Chapter Nineteen

Hunter

"How many guns are in this house?" Harlow's voice came off a little too harsh for my liking. She knew we needed them, so why was she only just now asking about it? I turned to her after I closed the door behind Bennett. She was standing with her arms crossed and her head tilted to the side. I glanced over at Jagger, lifting an eyebrow.

"Not my house," I said, pointing out the obvious. Harlow furrowed her brows, then turned to look at her brother. Good thing she realized we were standing in her own four walls.

"How many?" she asked, trying to sound just as serious as she did the first time. Jagger couldn't help a grin and I was close to mimicking his face since seeing Harlow like that was more cute than scary.

"Just a bunch," he told her, then got up from his seat to get himself another beer from the kitchen. Harlow wasn't happy with that answer, walking straight to the couch Bennett sat on minutes ago, lifting the cushion and picking up the handgun hiding underneath.

"How many? she repeated.

"Jesus Christ," I said as she waved the gun around like it was a toy. I walked over to stand behind her, reaching for the gun and taking it from her. "I hate to break it to you, sweetheart, but these things are dangerous."

"Yeah, no shit," she mumbled, crossing her arms over her chest again. I raised an eyebrow at her choice of words. It was amusing, yet this had to be taken seriously. I heard a chuckle from the kitchen and I looked up to see Jagger taking a sip from his beer, leaning against the doorway. "I'm all for hiding dangerous shit from her, but I kinda like this. Her getting all annoyed with you and talking back."

I rolled my eyes, putting the gun back down on the couch and covering it with the cushion. "I don't need her to get hurt. She can get as sassy with me as she wants." I sat back down, running my hands through my hair.

"Nobody answered my question," Harlow said, now sounding less interested in the number of guns laying around.

"Seven," was all Jagger said before sitting back down on the recliner. Harlow let out a sigh, letting herself plop down next to me.

"So, what now?" she asked, changing the subject.

"I won't stop working just because Dean is around," Jagger said, leaning back and looking at me. "He said there's another guy watching him, and

Dean can't be in two places at once. So as long they're watching him, we can go on with our lives."

"And what if he somehow finds a way to shake them off?" Harlow asked, looking concerned.

"Then Bennett did a shit job. Listen, Low," he said with a sigh. "I know you're scared. But staying in and stopping our lives because of that piece of shit is not gonna happen. He won't get that power over us. Not this time."

Harlow nodded, then turned to look at me. Her eyes were glassy, and I could tell she was on the verge of letting go some tears. "I don't want to stay in here because of him, either." And I knew what that meant. She had her job and she liked to work. She was also pretty damn safe in that diner unless Dean decided to go in. So, all I could do was to accept that offer. I ran my hand over my face before propping my elbows onto my knees, letting my head down. "I guess those people at the diner will have to get used to a new cook."

Harlow squealed, hugging me from the side with a huge smile on her face. "Thank you!" she said, happier than ever.

"So that shit was real?" Jagger asked. I looked up at him, putting my arm around his sister's back and pulling her closer to my side.

"Yeah," I said, now looking at Harlow. "She once asked me if I wanted to take on a normal job. You know, to cover just like you. So, now I have a reason to work there. I'll take care of her and make some more money I don't need."

Harlow rolled her eyes. "Ever thought about

giving it to charity?" she asked. Jagger and I both nodded. "They check where the money came from. They don't take any checks without a background check and our money is pretty much worth shit when it comes to charity," I told her.

"But we got some people we know who need some help to stay alive. We give some to them each month," Jagger added.

***

Harlow

And just like that, all the wrongs from being hitmen just disappeared. I knew they were just doing their jobs, helping other people out by killing others—God, that just sounded wrong. But I wasn't going to interfere in their lives. At least, knowing that they gave back to others was something positive.

"And I pay Bliss's rent. Least I can do after what she did for me as a kid." I smiled at Hunter, nodding.

"That's very sweet of you," I told him.

"Speaking of the devil," Jagger muttered while looking out of the window, letting his head fall back against the headrest. I turned to the window and saw Bliss get out of her car, her arms carrying two large paper bags with the logo of the diner she worked at on them.

"It's Bliss," I pointed out, getting up to go open the door. Hunter pulled me back down though, getting up himself and walking to the front door to open it for her sister. I took a glance at Jagger, who looked rather annoyed. What was the matter with them?

"Hey, Hun," Bliss said in her usual happy voice. No matter how loud she was, she did light up a room with her mood. "I hope you guys are hungry because I brought the best chicken wings in town." I turned to look at her, then got up to hug her. Hunter had taken the bags from her, setting them down on the couch table.

"Hello, darlin'," she said and hugged me back with a huge smile on her face.

"Hi," I simply said, enjoying the hug a little too much. Having a friend was nice.

When I stepped back to look at the food Hunter was taking out of the bag, Bliss turned to Jagger and pouted. "If I had known you'd be here, then I would've just dropped the food at the doorstep and left." She was teasing him, and I was just a little confused as to why she was mocking him like that. Jagger rolled his eyes, sitting up straight and reaching for a box of wings.

"Good to see you, Bliss," he told her.

I looked at Hunter and he shrugged, giving me a quick smile. Was I not reading them correctly? Did I miss something? Clearly, they had a thing for each other just some days ago and now he was all annoyed. I sat back down next to Hunter, still eyeing my brother and Bliss.

"Eat," Hunter whispered, telling me I should let go of all the thoughts surrounding the other two.

Oh, well. As long as they don't start a fight everything's fine. Still, it was amusing, yet confusing.

CHAPTER TWENTY

Harlow

I felt some tension in the room. Hunter and Jagger ate quietly, giving each other almost annoyed looks and Bliss kept on talking about her new man, Kit. She was mostly talking to me since I was the only one asking questions, but I could tell Jagger was listening. He rolled his eyes multiple times and that's when I realized what was going on. The last time he acted like this was at the diner, when Bliss told us the story of her exes and other guys she met in her life. Oh, my God. My brother was jealous. Because of Bliss.

I must've made a surprised face when I finally got the gist of it because Hunter chuckled and shook his head. "Welcome aboard," he whispered, letting me know he knew about them already. I glanced over at Jagger, who was now cleaning his hands with a wet wipe. He was pissed, ready to leave the living room. I looked back at Hunter, pressing my lips together tightly.

Even if I wanted to know more about Bliss and Jagger's romance, or whatever it was they had, it didn't feel right to just randomly ask. They obviously kept it secret and I didn't want to bother them about it. Bliss seemed to have it all under control anyway, making him jealous of the new guy she met some nights ago at a bar.

I had to let it go. It wasn't my business.

"Excuse me," Jagger said and got up from the recliner, taking his paper plate with the clean bones on it over to the kitchen. Hunter got up too and followed him with his plate. They started talking quietly, Hunter looking rather concerned.

"Anyway, I'm seeing him again tonight. So, I'll have to leave soon," Bliss told me with a smile that definitely didn't meet her eyes.

"Will you be okay?" I asked. I wasn't sure why, but something just didn't feel right. She didn't seem too enthusiastic about meeting that guy. It was either because of Jagger's lack of interest in Bliss now, or Kit was treating her badly and she just went to prove to Jagger that she didn't care about him either. That's complicated.

"Of course I will be okay. You should come out with me sometime."

"No," both Jagger and Hunter said, turning to look at us. Bliss raised an eyebrow.

"Why not?" she asked, looking rather confused. "She's almost twenty." She looked back at me with a smile. "And I know it's your birthday in exactly five days."

***

101

Hunter

Fucking hell. The first of October. How could I ever forget? Sweet Harlow was turning twenty and I didn't even buy a gift. The best thing about this was that Jagger once told me about her birthday. Harlow never talked about it, probably not wanting anyone to buy her gifts, but she was my girl and I wanted her to have a special day. I'd have to talk to Bliss about this. I wasn't really romantic, but I needed something to make it memorable for Harlow.

"Dean is in town. She can't go out. It's not safe," Jagger said in a low voice, sounding incredibly exasperated.

"It's not like she'll be alone," Bliss said. I crossed my arms and leaned back against the kitchen counter.

"We can't risk anything," I told her, hoping she would just let it go. Besides, Harlow didn't seem to find the idea of a club or bar amusing or intriguing.

"Would I even get in?" Harlow asked.

"Doesn't matter. You're staying with us. Either with him or me." Jagger was being clear, and I could tell he was trying to piss Bliss off this time.

My sister rolled her eyes, looking back at Harlow. "Someday we'll have some nice girls' night out, okay?"

Harlow nodded with a smile. "Sounds fun," she said, not really meaning it.

Bliss then got up and cleaned up the rest of the things on the coffee table. "I'll see you guys around," she said, kissing my cheek, giving Jagger a quick nod, and hugging Harlow goodbye.

When she left, Harlow glanced over at her brother. "Why are you so mean to her?"

Jagger raised a brow, letting out a laugh. "I'm not being mean. She's just a pain in the ass." And with that, he took another beer and walked toward his room. "Don't be too loud." He closed the door to his bedroom.

Harlow's eyes were full of questions and I couldn't help but chuckle. "As much as it bothers me, I'm not gonna ask any further questions. It's their problem."

Harlow studied me for a while, tilting her head to the side. "Doesn't it bother you that he called her a pain in the ass?" she asked.

I shrugged. "It's true."

Harlow sighed, getting up from her spot on the couch and walking over to me. I pulled her into my arms, kissing the top of her head as she leaned into me with her arms around my waist. "You should've reminded me about your birthday next Tuesday," I whispered, running my hand up her back and into her hair.

"I don't like my birthdays," she said quietly. "Jagger and I usually just get some cupcakes and that's it. Besides, I never really had people to invite to my birthday."

I hated the thought of Jagger not getting her more than just cupcakes for her birthdays. I knew he was hiding the fact that he killed people for a living, but Harlow deserved more than just lousy small cakes which were probably not even that good.

"You got me now. And Bliss." I pondered for a while before continuing. "I'll make some dinner.

And before that, we'll make ourselves a fun day. Maybe head out of town, get you some presents."

"I work on Tuesday," she said, keeping her voice still quiet.

"You got work tomorrow, right? I'm going with you and tell Frankie about wanting to work there and that we're gonna take a day off on Tuesday for your birthday." I was starting to think that she really hated her birthday. She didn't answer, instead, she lifted her head and revealed a small pout on her lips before kissing me. Great. Now she was just distracting me from my plan.

"Don't think we're done talking about your birthday," I whispered against her lips and pulled her closer. Her arms loosened around me and her hands coming up to hold on to my shoulders.

Just as I thought this would turn into yet another hot make-out session with my girl, she pulled back and looked up at me with a sweet smile on her face.

"I gotta get ready for bed," she said and walked off to the bathroom without saying another word.

CHAPTER TWENTY-ONE

Hunter

I had already slipped under the covers when Harlow came into the bedroom. She was wearing a long-sleeved shirt which she always wore to bed. It was too big on her and I wondered if it was just Jagger's. But then, even for Jagger, it would be too big.

"It's Dean's," she said quietly, noticing me staring at her shirt. I looked up at her, furrowing my brows in confusion.

"Why do you have that?" I asked, reaching for her hand and pulling her onto the bed next to me. She didn't hesitate but slid right under the covers next to me and snuggled up to my side. "I found it some years ago in a box we had lying around the house. Not sure why I kept it."

I cupped the side of her head with my left hand and held her close to my body with my other arm wrapped around her back. Of course, I didn't have an explanation for that either.

"It's just a sweatshirt," I said, thinking that I just stated the obvious, but she was probably thinking too much into it. Harlow nodded and turned her head to look up at me.

"When's your birthday?" she asked, changing the subject smoothly but bringing up something I'd rather not talk about.

"Not sure," I admitted, hoping this conversation would be over already. With a confused look on her face, she pushed herself up to look down at me.

"What do you mean you don't know?"

I shrugged, not meeting her eyes. "You think my parents left anything at the orphanage when they dropped me off there?" That came out a little harsh and I wished I had my temper under control. At least with Harlow. But as always, she stayed calm, trying to keep the conversation going without making me mad.

"So then…if they didn't leave any sort of birth certificate, how did you get your name?" she asked, and it was a legitimate question. I didn't give her much information other than my parents not leaving anything behind when they abandoned me.

Taking a deep breath, I prepared myself for what came next. "When they brought me to the orphanage, they had put a note inside the blanket I was wrapped in. The name Hunter was written on it, but I doubt that was the name they picked out for me. Who the fuck names their kid Hunter? Besides, there were no records in any hospital for a mother who birthed a baby named like that."

I was already starting to get angry, just remembering my past.

"I like it. I think it fits you," Harlow said with a smile, brushing some of my hair off my forehead. "And what about your last name?" She didn't linger too long on mt last answer.

"Kane is Bliss's last name. I didn't have any real identity, so they chose to give me the same name as her."

Harlow's smile never faded, and I could almost read her mind. She thought it was a good idea that they had given me Bliss's last name since we got to the orphanage on the same day. "I think your name is perfect. And Bliss is obviously proud of it," she said, confirming what I thought she was thinking.

***

Harlow

He let out a hard laugh, shaking his head and pushing me off to the side gently so he could sit up. "I couldn't care less what Bliss thinks about all that. Hell, I'm no one. My whole identity was pretty much made up by strangers, giving me a surname of a family I have nothing to do with." He was angry, and at that moment I couldn't do much other than listen and hope he'd calm down.

He started to pace the floor next to the bed, running his hands through his hair. "I have a fucking ID with a name on it that docsn't belong to me." He suddenly seemed concerned and stressed at the same time and I could tell by the way his bottom lip trembled that he was about to cry.

"Hunter…" I said quietly, getting up from the

bed and standing right in front of him, making him stop in his tracks.

"No," he said through gritted teeth. His eyes were darker than ever, and he was tense all over his body. The way he clenched his jaw told me he was keeping it all in.

"Hunter," I tried again, lifting my hands to cup his face. And just like that, his head fell, and a sob escaped him.

This was new to me. He had shown me many emotions throughout the past months but never had I seen him this frustrated and angry with *himself*. All I knew was that I hated to see him like that. He was bringing himself down, making himself feel bad and no one ever deserved to feel that way.

"I'm nothing," he whispered and that broke my heart.

"You're everything to me," I started, looking into his eyes and keeping his head between my hands so he wouldn't look away. "It might not be enough, but for me you're everything. Do you hear me? You're a good man and I've learned to love you the way you are. The person you are. You're perfect and I hate seeing you like this." I stopped for a second to gather all my thoughts. Seeing Hunter cry and suffer hurt.

"We break sometimes for things we didn't do. Things we're not guilty of. But what matters is what we do with our lives to change the way we felt in the past. I know this isn't about me, but no matter what Dean or my mother did to us, I don't let that shape me for who I wanna be today, or in five years." I was trying to prove a point, but it felt as if

I was just talking random things that didn't make any sense.

"What I'm trying to say is," I sighed, wiping away the tears on his cheeks. "I love you. I don't care what your name is, where you're from, or what those people did to you in the past. I love you for who you are."

Hunter didn't say a word at first. He just looked at me and small sobs escaped him. Finally, after a long, silent break of words being spoken, he sighed and pulled me to him with his hand on the back of my head and kissed me gently. "I love you too, sweetheart."

Thank God, because I wasn't letting go of him, ever.

CHAPTER TWENTY-TWO

Hunter

It felt good to just let go and let the emotions run out of me. I felt drained inside, wanting that emptiness in me to just disappear. Luckily, I knew Harlow was filling it slowly with her love. But I hated the way I still showed her my miserable sides. The ones I was trying so hard to hide from her and her beautiful soul. She didn't deserve the way I acted when I got angry, but I had yet to find out how to stop it.

Harlow handled me well when I went apeshit over the simplest things. Problem was, most things bothered me and the only way I was able to handle them was by getting angry. Harlow had asked me many times if I would like to talk about the things bothering me, but I always refused, knowing talking about those things only made me more anxious. That's why I had asked her to just let me burst and be patient. She was good at being patient with me— it was one of many reasons why I knew she was my one.

Anxiety was the other thing standing in my way to find real happiness. Of course, when Harlow was around, she was all that mattered. But the second she left, something like panic rose inside of me and all I wanted to do was either get her back in my arms or take out my gun and just shoot at a tree for several hours. Dealing with that shit was incredibly hard. People liked to make fun of those who suffered from depression and anxiety attacks. Nothing fun about that at all. All of that mixed up with the storm inside my head was hard to deal with.

Luckily, I had three people by my side who knew how to handle it all. People I knew I could trust blindly. One of those people was running her hand through my hair, making me shiver with her soft touch. We were still standing in the middle of her bedroom, my arms around her body, pressing her tightly against mine.

***

Harlow

What Hunter went through was serious. Bliss had talked to me about it before and she told me that he wasn't letting doctors help him. He said those doctors were bullshit and only treating people to make a *shit ton of money*. I've heard about some psychiatrists who didn't take their patients seriously, but I've also heard of some people getting better from therapy.

I was all for helping him learn to love himself and get better, but he refused to go see a doctor. For now, I was okay with it. I knew how to react to his outbursts and how to calm him down, but if it stopped working, I would talk to him about seeing a doctor. He told me he was doing okay, and I trusted him.

"We need some sleep," I whispered against his lips. The kiss he gave me turned into something more and his hands moved to my lower back, pressing his hips against me to let me feel his stiffening cock.

"I need you," he said in a hoarse voice which almost broke my heart. He knew how to use his words to make me melt, and lucky him, it worked every damn time.

His hands moved lower to cover my bottom, moving me against him to feel his thickness in his briefs. I rubbed up against him, wanting to feel more. As if he could read my mind, his hands slid down my thighs and then jerked me up by the knees until I couldn't help but wrap both my legs tightly around his hips. He moved to the bed, laying me down onto it and leaning over me with one arm propped up next to my head. We never broke the kiss, letting our tongues play with each other in soft, passionate movements.

His hardness was pressing against me where I needed it the most and I cried out against his lips, lifting my hips to meet his movements. Even with some of our clothes on, I still enjoyed this. He took his time, made me feel incredible, and always made sure I was the one getting pleasured first. He wasn't selfish. He cared.

"Fuck," Hunter muttered and broke the kiss, looking into my eyes while his left hand made its way down to my panties. My shirt was easily lifted to my stomach, revealing the black piece of fabric I wore underneath. Hunter never complained about the way I dressed, including my underwear. Bliss once showed me her collection of bras and slips. They were all different colors, some red, some black, and even a pink set. She explained how much guys liked girls in lingerie. At first, I thought I'd have to get something like that too. But then I asked Hunter about it, and if he would like to see me in that kinda stuff.

He just looked at me with a raised brow and told me, "Only gonna rip that shit off of you and get you naked anyway."

Remembering that conversation made me smile and I reached for his hand. His fingers were already on my panties, pushing them down my legs. "What's wrong?" he asked and stopped moving. I shook my head, pressing my lips together.

"I just love you, that's all."

He smiled at that, lowering his head to kiss my neck. He trailed kisses down to my collarbone, then lifted my shirt further and over my breasts. His lips touched my stomach and I couldn't stop watching him. When he licked along the hem of my panties, he finally tore them off of me and put them next to him on the bed. With one last glance, he lowered his head between my legs and let his tongue run over my most sensitive spot.

Another cry escaped me, and I couldn't help but

pull his hair tight. My hips buckled and that sweet sensation came over me. It wasn't just the way he flicked his tongue against my clit, but the way he held me tight with his hands on my stomach and thighs made it all feel incredible.

His eyes met mine and I felt the heat come over me as his tongue moved faster. "Oh, Hunter!" I moaned, lifting my hips again to let him know I was close. But then, I knew he felt it. I was shaking and I felt that familiar throb deep down my abdomen.

"That's it, love," I heard him say and I knew I was already on the edge of spiraling out of control. "Come for me. Let me taste your sweet pussy coming."

"HUNTER!" I finally cried out, throwing my head back and closing my eyes tightly. I was shaking, my legs trying to squeeze together and my toes curling against the bedsheets.

I was in heaven, and I was only realizing that it was just the beginning.

CHAPTER TWENTY-THREE

Hunter

When it came to Harlow and making her feel good, I didn't care about much else. I was focused on her and her body. The way she reacted to my touch and the sounds of my name falling from her lips. I was just as lost in all of it as Harlow was, and I shouldn't have been.

The slamming of the front door was enough to tell me that we had been too loud, letting Jagger take part in all of our private business. Fuck me.

I quickly got up from the bed and put on my jeans, which I'd folded carefully just moments ago before getting into bed. When Harlow realized what was going on, her face turned white and pure fear danced in her eyes. "Stay here. I got this," I told her, putting on a shirt before walking out of the room.

Before I reached the front door, I heard footsteps behind me, and I cursed at Harlow's lack of listening. I glanced back at her, frowning and

115

shaking my head. "Didn't you hear me?" I asked. She mimicked my expression and passed me to get to the door.

"This is my fault. I don't need you two to throw punches again."

With that, she stepped outside but stopped in her tracks when she saw Jagger pacing the small walkway leading up to the few steps we were now standing on.

"Harlow, let me talk to him," I whispered, taking her hand and pulling her back. By the look of it, Jagger was mad. The deep, long pulls he took from his cigarette told me he needed more than just a small thing like that to release some stress.

"No," she said and pulled her hand out of mine with one firm tug. I watched her leave the deck of the house, using the small steps and then walking up to Jagger. I ran my hands through my hair, knowing this time he wouldn't hold back. Not even on his sister. He was pissed and he was going to let it out right there.

***

Harlow

What was I thinking? I should've kept quiet and hid what we were doing in my bedroom. Even if Jagger told me he was okay with Hunter and me together, the thing we did a few minutes ago wasn't necessary for him to hear. I was ashamed and I hated the way I was feeling.

I've seen Jagger mad before, but never because

of me. It was either because of Dean, or something that happened at work. He talked to me about it and then that subject was cleared. But this time, I was the one who caused all of this. I made him mad.

I was standing right in front of him, but he didn't pay any attention to me. I was trying to form words for a good enough apology, but nothing came to mind. I was still stuck by the thought of him hating me. Luckily, he saw the struggle I had and started the conversation.

"I thought I was okay with this," he said, now turning to me and pointing at Hunter. "But this is too fucking much." He took the last drag from his cigarette before tossing it to the ground and lighting another one.

"Jagger, I'm sorry—"

"Shut it for a second, all right?" he said, looking at me with glassy eyes. He was tired and he also had work tomorrow, but I was keeping him up. I opened my mouth to argue back, to tell him not to talk to me that way, but I had no right to fight back now.

"Come on, man, don't talk to her like that," Hunter said calmly, yet his voice was serious. Jagger let out a harsh laugh, turning away from me completely.

"What'ya gonna do about it?" Jag said mockingly and took another drag. "Wanna fight me? Wanna end up with another broken nose like that time you let some bastard run over my sister?"

"Jag…" I cried out, letting a deep crease appear between my brows. Tears stung my eyes and I wondered why this was happening. Why now? We had enough shit to handle.

"Watch it, Jagger," Hunter warned and stepped closer. He pulled me back so I was standing behind him.

"Why, huh? Why the fuck would I watch it when you're fucking my sister in the next room?" I hated this. Hearing it made me feel sick. It was wrong, but it happened. Yet, I felt ashamed.

Jagger moved closer, not caring about any personal space. This wasn't going to end well. "Please, stop." I tried to step between them, but both of their arms pushed me back, not breaking their eye contact.

"We're sorry. Jesus, we're in love. What else do you expect?" Hunter said. That was the first time I slightly disagreed with him. Not the love part, but the fact that Jagger had to expect us having sex, or for that matter foreplay, when he's in the house.

"Hunter, please," I begged, trying to get both of their attention.

"It's my fucking house," Jagger roared, throwing his cigarette to the floor and pushing Hunter against his chest. He stumbled back a few steps but caught himself, standing back up straight.

"Don't start this, man," Hunter warned, holding up his hands to tell Jagger he's not going to push back. That's a start. Not much I was able to do at that point.

"This is bullshit," Jagger mumbled and shook his head, then took a swing at Hunter. I held my breath and closed my eyes for a split second to not witness what would happen next.

"Jesus Christ," I heard Hunter say and I looked back up at him, relieved at the sight of his unpunched face. He must've dodged Jagger.

"Stop!" I shouted, trying once again to step between them. They still ignored me and I was so damn close to just screaming until they paid attention to me. I didn't want to wake up the whole neighborhood, though. The ones who weren't already awake, that was.

"Are you done now?" Hunter asked, keeping his distance from Jagger.

"Are you done playing this game? She's fallen for your shit already. Stop fucking my sister in my damn house now." Jagger's words sounded rough. Every single one of them hit my heart hard, making me hold my breath. I could tell he was saying all that just to make Hunter angry. Jagger was looking for a fight and that's the only way he got one.

Hunter was tense. He was holding it all in, for my sake. I knew that much. "I'll stop fucking your sister when you stop fucking mine."

My jaw dropped and I was scared to move. This was getting messier every second.

Jagger's face fell and it seemed as if he forgot everything that had just happened. He frowned, realizing his secret wasn't so secret anymore, then he shook his head and turned away, walking toward his car. "Whatever," he said quietly, then opened the car door, ready to step in.

I ran after him, wrapping my hands around his arm and pulling him to me. "Where are you going?" I asked, confused. He tried to shake me off but I held onto his sweatshirt.

"Nowhere," he said and tried to push me away.

"I'm not letting you go without you telling me

119

where you're going."

"Nowhere," he repeated, then took a glance at Hunter before looking down at me. "I'll be back in the morning," he told me quietly, then he got into his car and drove off.

I watched as his car disappeared in the darkness, leaving me standing there in the cold fog. I felt Hunter coming up behind me, taking my hand carefully. "He'll be fine," he whispered and pulled me back toward the front door.

I knew he was safe, but it still hurt to see him leave like that. I'd never felt that way and I hated it.

CHAPTER TWENTY-FOUR

Hunter

Harlow was hiding her face, silently crying and pouring herself a glass of water at the sink. Her back was turned to me and I wasn't sure how to approach her after seeing the hurt expression on her face as Jagger drove off. I leaned against the doorway to the kitchen and crossed my arms over my chest.

Quiet sobs escaped her, and I could see the tension on her body rising. She was blaming it all on herself and that wasn't right at all. But that's just Harlow. No matter how wrong the other person was, she always felt like she had to be the one making it all right again. It was a beautiful trait but fucking stupid in this situation.

Sure, we were too loud, but she wasn't the only one taking part in what we did. And Jagger overreacted. The things he said were also not triggered by hearing her sister scream my name. Something else was bothering him and he just let all his frustration out on us. Never actually experienced Jagger acting all fired up.

When Harlow finally moved, she turned to look at me for a second before checking her phone for a message from her brother. The tears on her face kept on coming and the pain in her eyes was visible from miles away. It was heartbreaking seeing her like that, but then I wondered if there were any way this beautiful girl could ever see the bad in people. Jagger treated her like shit back then and she probably thought she deserved it. Fucking hell.

"He's not answering. And he hasn't seen my texts either," she said with a trembling voice. I sighed, stepping closer to her and taking her phone in my hand. I put it on the dining table next to me and then cupped her face with both my hands.

"He's fine. He just needs some time, all right? He's just upset, and he needs to calm down."

I tried my best not to talk too much or say something that would upset her. I knew Jagger had some guns in his car and he knew how to deal with people who try to start a fight.

"But what if Dean finds him?" she asked in a small voice. I shrugged.

"That's why Bennett's around. Come on, we gotta get some sleep. I bet Jagger will be home in the early morning and everything will be back to normal. He's thrown his fit and now he'll get over it."

Harlow studied my face, almost as if she were trying to see if she could trust me. "Okay," she whispered and reached up to brush the back of her hands over her cheeks to wipe away the tears.

"Now, go ahead. I'll make you some tea. Helps you sleep better."

She nodded her head, then with one last glance at the phone, she left the kitchen. When she was out of sight I walked over to the living room and picking up my phone, I sat down on the couch table and unlocked it to open my sister's chat.

Hunter: Is Jagger with you?

Bliss: Yes

Hunter: Is he all right?

Bliss: Pretty upset. He's been crying. Did something happen?

Hunter: No. Just let him know Harlow's upset too.

Bliss: Hunter…what's wrong? Hun?

Hunter: We'll have a talk about your little secret another time.

It seemed pretty damn necessary to let her know we all knew about her and Jagger and I was satisfied enough to just put the phone down and go make my girl a cup of tea. When I entered the bedroom, I saw Harlow curled up on the bed, her head next to the pillow and the covers all over the bed but not on her body. Somehow, it was the most adorable thing I had ever seen.

Her eyes were closed but I could tell she was awake by the way she hiccupped and frowned.

"I don't like crying," she muttered, and I couldn't help but smile.

"Then don't," I simply said and set down on the edge of the bed, holding the warm cup in my hand tightly. "Come on. It's not too hot, so you can drink it already." I took her hand in mine. "Sit up."

She did as I said and took the cup from me with both her hands, then slowly took a sip with her eyes on mine. "Jagger's with Bliss." I couldn't keep it from her. I knew where he was, and I didn't like Harlow all nervous and worried. Her eyes lit up immediately.

"Did you talk to him?" she asked, eyeing my body to check if I had my phone with me. I shook my head.

"I texted Bliss. She said he's fine and he'll be back tomorrow. Now, drink some more and then we gotta sleep.".".

***

Harlow

Nine a.m. came quickly. I wasn't very fond of sleeping only a few hours, but last night was incredibly painful for me. I was probably just overreacting, but never in almost twenty years had I felt so incredibly empty because of Jagger. He was my safe place for all those years and then seeing him drive off angry pulled something out of my chest, ripping it apart right in front of my eyes.

Dramatic, but true.

Hunter was surprisingly energized and was ready before I got dressed after my shower. He even made coffee. It was another rainy morning and I could hear low thunder outside. Not sure why, but those kinds of mornings made me feel protected and safe.

I put on my work uniform and tied my hair into a high ponytail, just how Frankie expected from me. As I walked out of the bathroom, I heard Hunter talk on the phone. Before I could reach the kitchen, he pushed the phone into his front pocket and let his eyes wander all over my body.

"Who was it? Jagger?" I asked, hoping to hear some news. Hunter didn't answer me but instead, he shook his head in disapproval. "First thing I'll ask Frankie is to change those damn outfits. Too fucking short. And it's freezing outside."

I let out a small laugh, shaking my head and holding up one of his sweaters he once let me borrow. "I got this to keep me warm on the way there. Besides, the diner's heated," I explained while putting on the sweater and hoped he would drop that topic as quickly as he picked it up.

He shook his head once again. "Don't care about that, love. It's too short."

I rolled my eyes and changed the subject. "Did you talk to Jagger just then?" I asked and took a step toward him to wrap my arms around his neck. He studied my face, then bent his head to kiss my lips.

"Work," he simply said, and I knew not to ask any more questions.

I let it slip, running my hands into his hair and

pulling him closer to me while his tongue asked for permission. I parted my lips, letting my tongue touch his and I had to make sure not to forget about work.

His hands moved slowly over my body and his kiss got gentler with every stroke of his tongue against mine. One thing I knew for sure. Hunter was able to make me forget certain things in those moments.

When his hands cupped my bottom, I couldn't help but smile and press myself against his body. "We gotta go to work," I mumbled into the kiss and to my surprise, he let go of me immediately.

"Too bad," he said mockingly and walked right past me without another word. I laughed and followed him out the door. With Jagger's car still being gone, I hoped I would see him later tonight when I got back home.

CHAPTER TWENTY-FIVE

Hunter

We arrived at the diner, and before getting out of the car, Harlow and I kept our discussion about her work uniform going. I hated how much skin was visible and how tight it was on her body. I wasn't trying to be the jealous guy, but I just couldn't help it.

"Isn't that uncomfortable anyway?" I asked, trying to keep my voice low.

"It's very comfortable," Harlow said and pulled on the handle to open the door again. I had locked the car so she wouldn't just walk away from this. "Hunter, I don't wanna be late," she said in a tight voice while her eyes went wide.

"Will you talk to Frankie about your uniform?" I asked. Harlow sighed and shook her head.

"Let me out or I won't talk to you for the whole day."

I grinned, finding it adorable rather than scary, the way she threatened me.

"I don't think so," I told her and lifted an eyebrow. "It's just the uniform I'm complaining about, Harlow." This was a stupid conversation to have at nine-fifty-three a.m., but I hated the thought of older men eyeing her right in front of me. That is if Frankie would give me the job, of course.

Harlow studied me for a while before throwing her head back and groaning, obviously annoyed with me. "I will talk to him about it, now let me go."

"Was that so hard?" I mocked and unlocked the doors for her to get out. She didn't respond with words, but her middle finger was right in my face before she slammed the door shut. I watched her walk over to the back entrance and unlock the door, then she looked back and raised her brows.

"Come on," she said and I couldn't bite back a laugh.

"Too fucking sweet," I said to myself and stepped out of the car to follow her.

Harlow led me through the back of the diner, passing some doors which were labeled as the toilet, closet, and basement. Before we reached the kitchen, Harlow stopped in front of an open door. I could smell a cigar and beer. I liked both those things, but it was too early for even me to consume them.

"Good morning, Frankie," Harlow said in a sweet voice, and now that I stepped behind her, I saw him sitting in a large chair behind a desk. He looked up and smiled tiredly, then got up to walk over to us.

"Morning, Low," he mumbled, then looked up at

me and eyed me before nodding once.

"Hunter, is it?" he said, and I nodded, holding out my hand for him to shake.

"Yes, sir." And at those words, I cringed. The only guy I had to call sir was that son of a bitch foster dad who took Bliss and me in. Shit times bring shit memories.

I shook the thought away and concentrated on the important things that were happening. "Harlow told me about your need of cooks. I could cover that," I told him and watched as Harlow left toward the kitchen. She probably thought this was my shit to deal with. Hell, and she was right.

Frankie studied me, taking his time to let my offer sink in. "Ever cooked for a big crowd?" he asked.

I shook my head. "Not really. But I don't think it's an obstacle. I'm a great cook."

I was probably being too confident, but I wasn't leaving without him giving me a try.

"We'll see about that. First day I won't pay you. If today goes well, you can come back tomorrow. Let Nixon introduce you to the kitchen," he said and turned to go back to his chair.

"Yes, sir."

***

Harlow

When our last cook quit, Frankie had to find another one to make sure we still had someone to prepare all the food. Frankie was lucky enough to talk his nephew into coming in until he found someone and now Nixon was showing Hunter around the kitchen, telling him what to do.

I loved how well Hunter cooperated and listened. Normally, being bossed around wasn't his thing and taking the lead was more likely to motivate him. Not this time, though, and I started to wonder if he kept it together just for me.

Of course, he didn't have many choices now. He was around to protect me from Dean. So, he had to make the best out of it.

It was around eleven a.m. when I grabbed some lunch for Frankie and myself from the kitchen, letting Hunter and Nixon talk and cook. They seemed to get along, which I never expected them to. Nixon was a rich kid, living his best life over in Grand Island. His parents owned some sort of business, and after finishing college, he just took some years off to do basically nothing. He told me he moved here to help out Frankie but will move back home as soon as Frankie had found someone to work full time.

"He's a good kid," Frankie said as I handed him his plate and sat down on the small couch in his office. I smiled, nodding my head.

"He's a great cook too. The people also seem to love the food. I got big tips," I told him.

Frankie nodded, then took a bite from his food. "You think he can work here every day? Nixon will probably leave when he finds out I'll keep Hunter. And I didn't get any more applicants yet."

There was one thing coming to mind when he asked about taking over the kitchen full time.

Hunter had his other job to attend, mostly by night. And sometimes he left for more than one day, and when he came back, he was tired or just not in his right mind. I mean, after killing someone, that's normal, right?

"Maybe I can talk to Nixon. Ask him if he'd be okay with staying a little longer," I suggested, and Frankie shrugged.

"You can try to convince him. He already got the hots for you, anyway."

Perfect. "I'll make sure he understands Hunter and I are together."

Frankie chuckled and shook his head. "Nixon thinks he's the greatest. He'll see Hunter as a challenge. Only thing bigger than his ego is his bank balance."

I laughed, knowing there was no way Hunter would even let it go that far. "I guess he'll just have to accept the fact that I'm Hunter's."

Frankie nodded and smiled, studying my face for several seconds. "He making you happy?"

"Very," I told him. "I don't think I have ever loved someone the way I love Hunter." Because he had my heart and I didn't want it back.

"You just make sure he keeps on making you happy. You're an amazing young woman and you know you're like a daughter to me. If he fucks up, I'll kill him with my bare hands."

I bit my bottom lip, trying not to smile like a fool. "Don't worry, Frankie. I know I got him all wrapped up around my finger."

Chapter Twenty-Six

Hunter

Nixon stopped explaining things to me after breakfast rush hour and just let me do my thing in the kitchen. He was helping me out, but he mostly was talking about his private life. Quite honestly, they were the most boring stories I'd ever heard in my life. He was living off his parents' money and didn't have a clue about his future. A lot of the time I had to hold back and make sure not to tell him to shut up and just do his work, but then I watched Harlow waiting the tables and everything else that bothered me vanished.

Frankie came into the kitchen from time to time to check on us, making sure to watch me for several minutes so I could prove to him that I was indeed a good cook. I knew what I was doing and didn't need any help. But still, working full time at this diner was impossible for me with Gunner calling me up almost weekly to assign a new job. I somehow needed to explain to Frankie that I couldn't take this job full time.

"I was worried you would be too distracted watching her work but you're actually doing a good job," Frankie said and leaned against the counter. I looked over at him, stirring the pot with the pasta in it.

"I'm more distracted by those guys eye-fucking my girl. You think there's something we can do about that uniform? It's too short." I knew it was up to Harlow to talk about it, but she was busy, and deep down I knew she wouldn't approach Frankie about it anyway.

"I like it," Nixon called out from next to the fridge and I gave him a serious look.

"Sure you do," I mumbled and turned to Frankie again. He shrugged and ran his fingers over his full beard. "She's earning more by wearing that shit. She works hard but she needs that money."

I almost laughed. Not because he thought she needs the money because not even Nixon could keep up with mine nor Jagger's bank balance, but it was almost insulting the way he thought that Harlow would only get tips by wearing a tight, short thing like that. I was positive that her face was enough to get those men hard, and Jesus Christ, just thinking about that made me wanna vomit.

Those men were in their late fifties and over and the fact that they came here to eat and get a little show was incredibly disgusting.

"I got her covered. She doesn't need those tips," I told Frankie and he shrugged again.

"It's up to her. If she wants to change it, she can do whatever. There's a thrift shop on St. Joseph

Avenue that sells old work clothes. You can find anything in there."

"Yeah, I once found a full cop uniform when I was a kid and it was the best day ever," Nixon chimed in and I swear to God, I was so damn close to picking up the boiling pot and throwing it at him. He was unbearable now.

Frankie and I ignored him, and I turned back around to check on the pasta. "I'll have a look around then." I was happy with how the conversation turned out and I couldn't wait to take Harlow there to buy a new uniform. If we couldn't find a good fit, I could always order a new one online.

***

Harlow

Knowing Hunter was there watching me work was pushing me to work harder. It was weird, but it motivated me. We didn't really talk much since we had a lot of people coming and going. I was running back and forth, trying to make all the customers happy and hoping I wouldn't mix up any orders.

Luckily, before dinner rush hour, Adeline came in to help. I hadn't seen her since the accident and I wasn't even sure if she would ever be back to work, but I was glad she was. I could use her help and I think Hunter was happy to finally give Nixon a distraction from me. Adeline was flirty with him and she ignored Hunter entirely. She knew he was mine and she was respectful enough, maybe even too much, to just make sure Nixon was having the day of his life.

It was around seven p.m. when most customers left and just a few started coming in to have a piece of cake or some ice cream. I took the chance to help with the dishes and let Adeline work upfront on her own. Nixon had enough for the day so he grabbed himself a can of soda and sat down at the counter to be able to talk to Adeline.

"I think today went well," I told Hunter when we were alone. I smiled up at him as he stepped closer to me to drop the dishes into the sink. He nodded with a tired smile and kissed my temple softly.

"Was great," he said and turned back to the stove, scrubbing away the residues.

"I think Frankie likes you too."

"Yeah, he said I got the job. Did you tell him about me not being able to work full time?" he asked and I nodded. "He just needs Nixon to stay until he finds someone else. But I think Adeline is reason enough for him to stay."

Hunter chuckled and turned back around to look at me. "That fucker's annoying as fuck. I just hope I get enough anger out at my other job before I get here."

I looked up at him and wrinkled my nose. "I hope so too."

Standing on my tiptoes, I gave him a quick kiss before continuing to clean the dishes. "I can't wait to get home," he told me, and I couldn't agree more.

"Harlow, your brother is here!" Adeline's voice called out and I immediately dropped everything into the water and walked out of the kitchen to see

Jagger standing next to the entry. He had his hands tucked into his pockets and the way he was dressed told me he was going somewhere later. He looked clean and his freshly shaven face looked good.

When I reached him, I wasn't sure what to do. I wanted to hug him, but I felt like he was holding back from even touching me. So, I stood still, right in front of him, pressing my lips into a thin line and thinking about what to say to him.

"Are you going out?" I asked, thinking it was the best thing to ask. Maybe he had a date. With Bliss. Jagger studied me for a while, then took a glance over at Hunter who I knew was watching us. When his eyes were back on mine, he nodded.

"I would like to have dinner with you. Talk and apologize," he said, and I suddenly felt release coming over me. I loved how much he put into this, but I wasn't sure he needed to do all that just because of what happened the night before.

"What do you think? Some alone time, just us. We haven't done something like this in a while." He was right. The last time we spent some brother-sister time together was long ago. Before Hunter happened.

How was I supposed to say no? "I'd love to." I was tired from working all day but if Jagger wanted to talk, I couldn't just reject him. I was eyeing him from head to toe and I was still holding back my need to hug him. I suddenly felt nervous, hoping last night didn't change anything between us.

A smile appeared on his face. "Come here," he whispered and pulled me into his arms. I suddenly felt the urge to cry. That was probably too annoying, so I kept it in but hugged him back tightly.

"Thank you for coming," I told him. "Always. Now, let me talk to Hunter really quick and then we'll leave." I nodded slowly, letting go of him and stepping aside to let Jagger walk over to the kitchen. I followed him and already took off the apron I'd put on to wash the dishes.

"You all right?" Hunter asked Jagger, looking concerned.

"Yeah," he responded and nodded toward me. "I'll take her to get some Mexican food. Gotta talk to her and then we'll be back home before midnight."

"What about Dean?" Hunter said more quietly. I was amazed by how well they both just forgot about their little fight last night and moved on with the more important stuff. *Men*, I thought.

"Bennett just texted me minutes ago. Dean's on the other side of town. They got their eyes on him so we'll be fine. You just…wait at home."

Hunter slowly nodded, knowing that Jagger meant our home. He smiled at me and kissed my forehead quickly. "Enjoy. I'll finish up here and meet you at home."

"Okay," I said and then looked up at Jagger. He nodded toward the door, leading the way. I quickly looked down at my outfit and didn't really mind the fact that Jagger was all dressed up. He put the effort in for me and I liked the way he looked. Bliss was lucky.

But then, I was luckier. I had him for life and that I knew for sure.

CHAPTER TWENTY-SEVEN

Harlow

The restaurant Jagger drove us to was crowded even that late in the evening. It was a popular Mexican place and I could tell by the smell of the food that it was going to be good. It was located just fifteen minutes from home and Jagger told me that we would be back early enough for me to get some sleep.

We sat down at our table and already ordered our drinks so we wouldn't spend too much time deciding. When the waiter came back with our drinks, we ordered our food since we already knew what we liked. Tacos, some nachos with cheese, and corn casserole.

"I know this food isn't supposed to make you forget the way I acted last night, but I thought it would be nice to come here and let you eat as much as you want. You know about the money and I shouldn't be so selfish and keep it from you, but I hope you understand the situation I'm in is a bit difficult," Jagger explained and talked calmly, making sure no one would hear him talk.

I shook my head at his fear of me not understanding his thought process. "It's okay, Jag. Money's not important to me."

"But it's your money. You earned it from working hard and I just kept it hidden from you. It's not fair and I hate how little you care about it." Jagger seemed frustrated and I could tell he wasn't mad at him, but at me for not wanting what he wanted to give me.

"We've talked about this before. As soon as your contract with Gunner ends, we will move and start over." But that didn't mean I would accept money from him I didn't earn myself. He didn't need to know that, though.

"Yeah, that's the plan," he simply said and sighed as our food was served. I thanked the waiter and then looked at Jagger with a smile.

"Thank you for this."

He nodded and gave me a smile back. "Anything for you."

We started eating and I wasn't sure if I had to ask him about last night or if he would just start talking about it on his own. Luckily, that question was answered shortly.

"I'm sorry for what I said. I know you guys are in love. I guess it's just hard for me to accept since he never really had any relationship with girls other than some one-night stands or shit like that. And I hated the thought of you having someone else by your side who wants to protect and love you."

Jagger's words made me want to cry of

happiness. He was incredibly sweet, and I just wished every single girl on this planet had a big brother like him.

"So, you're jealous of Hunter?" I asked in an attempt to lighten the mood a bit. He chuckled, shaking his head.

"My love is for eternity. It's different. It goes deeper than anything. Hate to say this, but you never know what will happen in a few years. But no matter what, I'll still be around."

I knew he wasn't trying to scare me by saying that Hunter and I could potentially someday split up, but that thought never crossed my mind. I knew what Jagger meant.

"And I guess the fact that he's my best friend makes it even harder for me to just accept it. Hell, you're my little sister. It was hard enough to deal with everything that happened to you as a kid and now my friend has fallen for you." He shook his head, then grinned. "Almost like a bad romance book."

We both laughed at that and I shook my head as well. "I hope we're not that cliché."

"I guess it's just something I'll have to get used to. He's a good guy. Love him like a brother, but if he hurts you, I'll make sure I get paid to kill him."

"He'll be good. He has changed, I think. Sometimes I feel like he's at peace with himself. And if he's not, he'll talk about it with me. And I bet he talks to you about it too. Or Bliss."

At the mention of Bliss's name, Jagger's eyes seemed to get darker, almost as if he was losing interest in something.

"I'm sorry. I didn't mean to…" I wasn't sure how to approach him about her. They obviously were seeing each other, but Jagger didn't seem very happy about it.

"It's fine. Just complicated, that's it."

"Do you want to talk about it?" I asked with a small smile. Jagger shrugged, then sighed deeply and ran his hand through his hair

"She's being a pain in the ass. Nothing more to say about it. We had some fun, but that's over now. She's a friend, I guess."

I knew girls were complicated and I was positive that ninety-nine percent of the time in situations like Jagger and Bliss, communication was not running smoothly. But I wasn't asking any further since he seemed uninterested in talking about it anymore.

"That's good to hear. I like her too," I told him. He nodded once, then started with his tacos.

"Is there anything you want to talk about? About Dean, maybe?" he then asked, and I wasn't sure if I even wanted to talk about it.

I shrugged, not sure what to say. "I just hope it all just ends soon. I want him to leave."

Jagger studied me for a while, then reached for my hand on the table, squeezing it lightly. "Me too. We'll just have to wait for him to mess up so the cops can take him away. Until then, we'll just do our best not to stop living because of that son of a bitch." I nodded, giving him a tight smile. I was hoping for Dean to fuck up as soon as possible. I felt nervous inside, knowing he was around and probably up to no good. But we were safe, I thought. With Bennett around, nothing could happen to either of us.

CHAPTER TWENTY-EIGHT

Hunter

Days passed and working at Frankie's was almost better than my real job. I enjoyed being around Harlow and watching her work. She knew she was good at what she was doing, and the diner guests adored her, even if most of them were damn close to receiving a fist straight into their faces.

I tried to push those needs aside and remembered how much Harlow loved this place. She stopped going to school a while ago and Jagger and I had a talk with her about the importance of a college degree. We quickly found out that Harlow, even with her smart mind, wouldn't keep on attending school and just drop out of it to work.

It was probably the wrong choice because it would be hard to get a real job without a college degree. But Harlow insisted on dropping out, telling us she knew what she was doing. She was being stubborn, but then, Jagger and I were the last two people to tell someone to finish college. Hell, we both stopped attending high school in our freshman year. Or, in my case, I never actually entered a high school building.

Harlow told us not to worry and that she knew where she was going in life. I hoped she also knew that if Frankie's Diner someday, for some reason, closed, she would have trouble finding a new job. She just shrugged and changed the subject.

It was October first and I was on my way to pick up Harlow. Luckily, not long after I started working at the diner, Frankie found another cook, some college kid in need of some money, and another waitress to cover some shifts so Harlow wouldn't have to work her ass off every day.

I showed up at work whenever I was free and didn't have to work for Gunner. It worked well that way and I was able to keep an eye on Harlow as much as possible.

Harlow took the day off on her birthday and the next day, so we could spend some alone time somewhere out of Hastings.

I spent the last day working and was able to get some hours of sleep and preparing everything for Harlow's birthday before picking her up at work at six.

Jagger was at the diner already, making sure Dean wouldn't show up, and that way they could spend some time together for her birthday too. I parked at the back of the diner and got out quickly, locking the door and walking through the backdoor.

Passing the kitchen, I nodded at the new cook, whose name was something like Eli or Elliott, then I reached the front and stood behind the counter. I let my eyes travel through the whole diner, recognizing people until my eyes met Harlow's.

They lit up and she got up from the table and ran toward me. I chuckled, letting her melt in my embrace when she reached me. "Happy birthday, my love," I told her between kisses, hugging her close to my body.

"I missed you," she whispered against my lips. I couldn't help but laugh since we'd seen each other just one day ago before I left for work. But truth was, I missed her too.

I leaned back to look at her face, brushing back the strands of hair from her forehead. "How was your day?" I asked, knowing she was working, but also was allowed to take some more breaks to talk to Jagger.

"Great! Frankie made me a cake. Jagger and I didn't eat all of it, so you can try some too," she told me and I looked over at the table. Jagger was sitting there with a pleased look on his face. I nodded toward him and looked back at Harlow.

"Let's go sit down before we leave," I said.

"You okay?" Jagger asked as I sat down with Harlow by my side. I nodded. "Gunner needs us for a job. Not sure how that's gonna work if no one's watching Harlow."

Harlow sighed. "Can't I just stay with Bliss? I mean, Bennet would call if something's off." I studied her for a while, knowing that Bliss's wasn't a safe place either.

"We'll find a way to make it work. You guys go ahead and have fun. Try to be careful, though." The last sentence was directed to me and I knew Jagger was talking about Dean. Anything could happen and we couldn't be sure if he wasn't going to follow us out of Hastings.

I hadn't told Harlow where we were going yet. It was a surprise and I hoped it was good enough for her birthday. She told me not to organize anything too big, and that she was okay with just dinner. But I couldn't do that. I wanted her to feel relaxed for once. She deserved it.

I was taking her to Sutton, a small town just thirty minutes away from Hastings. I booked a room at the Fox Hollow Motel, including a spa, dinner, and breakfast. It wasn't too fancy, but it had great reviews.

"You be careful too, okay?" Harlow told Jagger and stood up to hug him. "No need to worry about me, sweet girl." After their long hug, I promised Jagger to have her back home the next day around two.

"You ready?" I asked Harlow as we put our seatbelts on. She nodded with a big smile, looking over at me with bright eyes. "I'm excited to find out where we're going to spend the night. It's going to be amazing. How long until we're there?"

"It's a half an hour drive. Oh, and I got something for you," I said to her and turned onto the main road. "But you have to open it later when we're there."

Harlow wrinkled her nose and then nodded. "I don't like presents. Jagger got me an old record player. It's beautiful but I bet he spent a lot of money on it. I love it, though," she said with a smile.

"And did he get you any records to play?" I asked, reaching over to put my hand on her thigh.

She shook her head and started playing with my fingers on her lap. "No. But I can get them myself. He said he has no idea what type of music I like," she said with a laugh. I chuckled, threading my fingers through hers and glancing over at her quickly.

"So what will be the first record you'll buy?" I asked, already knowing the answer. "Probably R.E.M.," she said, puckering up her lips and studying my hand. "I think *Automatic for The People* was the very first full album I downloaded on my phone."

I nodded, remembering all the times she talked about the songs on that album, telling me how good they were. I didn't really listen to many artists, and most of them were either already dead or just not very well known. But Harlow's playlist was incredibly interesting. From rock music to indie, some rap, and even country.

"When we get back tomorrow, we can go check out the record store."

Harlow nodded in agreement and I was getting impatient, wanting to give her my present already.

CHAPTER TWENTY-NINE

Harlow

The motel parking lot was full of cars when we arrived, and I was surprised that Hunter didn't mind all those people at all. He explained to me that the motel had a golf course in the back and even a lounge with a pool and cocktail bar. He wanted to do something fun with me, he said, and I loved his idea. We never got to go out and have some fun, and even if I only turned twenty, I wanted to find out what it was like to go out and dance or have some drinks.

"You're not twenty-one yet, sweetheart. Alcohol's gotta wait," Hunter said after I asked him if I could get a cocktail.

I sighed and stepped on the small balcony of our room, looking over the pool area filled with young people dancing and having fun. "I had alcohol before. Besides, I bet half of those people down there are not allowed to drink either."

"I don't care about others. You're too young and

I know for a fact that Jagger wouldn't allow it, either," he said seriously. I rolled my eyes, turning to look at him while he unpacked the duffel bag with our clothes in it. We didn't bring much since we were only staying one night, but I wanted to look good tonight. For him.

"One drink. Just one," I begged, stepping closer to him and stopping in front of him. "It's my birthday," I pointed out, wrapping my arms around his waist to get his attention. He looked down at me, letting go of the pants he was holding in his hand and dropping them on the bed next to us.

A serious expression covered his face. "No."

"Hunter," I sighed, letting my head fall back while closing my eyes. "Come on." I looked back up at him and let my hands travel up to his shoulders, holding on tightly and pulling him closer. "Just agree on one drink and I won't bother you about it anymore."

Hunter let out a laugh, shaking his head and pushing me to the side to keep on unpacking. "Bother me all you want, love. You're too young for that shit and I don't need something to happen to you tonight."

I crossed my arms over my chest and eyed him for a while. "When did you become such a rule-follower? I thought you were more fun." I was mocking him now and my goal was clear: get at least one cocktail before going to bed.

"I am fun," he said in an almost hurt tone. I tried not to laugh and to sound just as serious as he did. "Hell, I'm a fun guy." Now, his expression was filled with confusion and he seemed offended.

"Not right now," I told him, holding back laughter. "Or else you would just let me drink."

Hunter looked at me and his expression changed immediately. "Stop it," he ordered, and a deep crease appeared between his brows. "I said no, and I won't change my mind. Now, sit down at let me give you my present."

I was messing with him and I soon remembered that I probably shouldn't. Hunter was quick to explode, and I could tell he was starting to lose his patience with me. There was nothing wrong with pushing him to his limits, but only if I knew how far I could go.

***

Hunter

"I didn't want a present," she said quietly and sat down on the edge of the bed. I knew she was trying to make me mad, see how far she could actually go by not accepting a simple no.

Sure, we were pretty much in a city no one really knew about and I was positive too that most of the kids down there weren't twenty-one yet. I didn't care about them though. When it came to Harlow, I wanted her to understand that even if I was doing illegal stuff, she shouldn't follow my lead. Or her brother's.

I wanted her clean and innocent. Well, as innocent as it could get after our many nights of ridiculously great sex.

"I know. But on birthdays, gifts are a must. Now,

close your eyes," I told her and waited until she stopped looking at me like she was mad and covered her eyes with her hands.

"No peeking," I said, and pulled out the present from the duffle bag. I had to hide it underneath my clothes, and I was glad she didn't look through the bag during the car ride.

"All right, you can grab it." I held the present in front of her and she reached out her hands, keeping her eyes closed. The second she held it in her hands she smiled, and I knew she would love it.

"Can I look?" she asked excitingly. I sat down next to her and nodded, even though she couldn't see me.

"Yes."

She opened her eyes, looking at the large thin square in her hands with a huge smile. "I think I know what this is," she said and then looked at me. "I think it's a vinyl record."

I chuckled and shrugged, not wanting to disappoint in case it was something different. But of course, it wasn't. "Open it," I said to her with a smile.

She didn't hesitate, ripping up the wrapping paper. Her eyes went wide when she saw what was written on the record and she suddenly seemed speechless. "How..." she stuttered, taking a good look at her first-ever vinyl.

"Hunter, how on earth did you get this?" she asked, obviously shocked. I shrugged, leaning back on my elbows.

"That's a secret," I told her with a grin and got a slap on my knee as a reaction to my answer.

"Hunter, I need to know if this was somehow illegally smuggled or stolen or if I can keep it with a good conscience."

I laughed and shook my head. "Oh, so now you're worried about the legal stuff?"

"Tell me," she ordered, still in shock and not taking her eyes off of her new R.E.M., *Automatic for the People* LP, which was signed by each band member. "This is the best thing ever and I need to know."

"I bought it. That record store I want to take you to tomorrow is filled with rarities like this one. The guy who sold it to me was the one who got it signed. He went to their concert in Phoenix, Arizona in 1995." That guy also wanted a fair amount of money for it, but it was the perfect present for Harlow. Hell, if that band was still going on tour, I would even go with her just to see her this happy.

"This is incredible," she whispered, her eyes now filled with unshed tears. For me, this was a small present. I should've gotten her something bigger, but for now, and with everything happening around us, I thought this was enough for now. And I knew she appreciated the smaller things more. She wasn't into money, which was one thing I adored about her.

"Thank you. I love it. And I love you," she said, turning to me and leaning toward me to kiss me. I returned her kiss, sitting back up and cupping her face in my hand to keep her close.

This was all I cared about. Her love and her being happy. She deserved the world and so much more. I often wondered what life would be without her. Just the thought of it made me feel empty. Luckily, I had her. For now, and hopefully forever.

CHAPTER THIRTY

Hunter

Initially, I wanted to have a nice dinner with Harlow before attending the party outside. I didn't know there would be so many people at this motel, but it didn't bother me. Harlow never got out and the sight of young people dancing and having fun was intriguing her. A lot.

So I decided to just skip the romantic stuff at dinner, thinking after the party ends I would get her all alone in bed, stripping her down naked and enjoying every little inch of her body.

It was her birthday, and other than the alcohol, there was nothing I wanted to keep from her tonight. Well, besides other guys. Some time ago I realized that I got jealous quickly as soon as some guy just tried to speak to her, even if she was just taking orders or greeting customers.

I tried to ignore those feelings, knowing she was mine and no one could ever take my spot.

The dress she was wearing didn't really help

though. It was hitting a few inches above her knees, getting tighter toward her hips and hugging her waist perfectly. She looked stunning with her hair down, long curls falling over shoulders and the bright smile she was wearing was the best thing about it all.

I noticed some guys staring at her, then the second I wrapped my arm around her waist, they turned their heads. Good. She's mine. Everyone should know.

We stood next to the bar and I looked around to find ourselves a table. I got myself a beer and for Harlow a sweet tea. The bartender didn't take his eyes off Harlow, asking her multiple questions about how her night was going. I was fine with him ignoring my presence, but I'd much rather have him ignore Harlow too. He didn't stop, instead, he kept on flirting with her right there, in front of me. Luckily, Harlow was visibly uncomfortable. I stared him down, telling him to give me my drinks and to fuck off afterward.

I heard Harlow chuckle, putting her hand on my back. "Be nice, Hunter. He's just being nice," she told me and fuck me, at this point in our relationship, she could tell me anything and I would obey her like a puppy.

I nodded toward a table and Harlow followed me to stand by it. There were several high tables around the pool, most of them filled with empty glasses and bottles. I pushed the ones on our table aside and made room for us.

"I don't really like the music," she said, looking around and taking a sip of her sweet tea. Her wrinkled nose told me that she not only didn't like the music, but she hated it with all her heart. A DJ was hired to take care of the mood for the party, but I couldn't agree more with Harlow. He played early 2000's music, mixed with some annoying EDM. Electronic dance music, my ass.

"We'll have to get through it. Or we can just leave and head up to the bedroom," I suggested, finding that option was a better way to spend the evening. Harlow shook her head, looking up at me with shimmering eyes. "No. Other than the music, everything's perfect."

I nodded and leaned over to kiss her temple. "You look stunning," I whispered, needing her to hear it from me first before some random guy decided to hit on her. They were all still looking at her, acting like I wasn't around suddenly.

"You're handsome as well," she said with a smile and ran her fingers over my shirt. "White suits you." She pressed her lips against mine. I loved black clothes. But I wanted to change it up for once. White was my only option.

I returned her kiss, pulling her closer to make sure everyone saw that she's mine. To make it even clearer, I cupped her ass into my hands and squeezed tightly, making Harlow moan with surprise. She liked it, pressing her body against mine and wrapping her arms around my neck. Her hands made their way into my hair, pulling them tightly to simulate my hands on her bottom.

My tongue touched her bottom lip and she opened her mouth for me to deepen the kiss. With our tongues twirling around each other and our hands not stopping from touching, I couldn't care less about the people watching. Hell, I wanted them to watch. The caveman in me was trying to get out again, but I wasn't going to push this any further. If I kept going, I'd pick her up to run upstairs to the bedroom to make sure the need I knew was growing between her thighs was getting its satisfaction.

She wasn't making it easy on me since my cock started growing inside my pants. Her hands grabbed fistfuls of my hair, slowly making me crazy. I loved the way she touched me, knowing exactly what I liked.

I needed to slow down, so I put both hands on either side of her waist, yet still holding her tight. "Wanna dance?" I mumbled into the kiss. Her lips left mine in an instant and surprise was all over her face.

"You dance?" she asked, not quite believing me.

I chuckled, nodding my head and straightening out her dress to make sure it didn't ride up more. "I'm not the best, but I want to dance with you," I told her, nodding toward our drinks. "But we gotta drink up first. Don't need anyone to put shit into your drink."

Harlow grabbed her drink, downing it like a pro and then grinned up at me. "Come on!" Her excitement could probably be seen from miles away. I finished my beer, then took her hand and pulled her to what seemed to be the dance floor right next to the pool. When we found a good spot, I pulled her close again and started moving to the awful music coming from the speakers.

The way Harlow moved made me regret the

decision to dance. Her hips swayed from side to side and her ass looked better than ever in that dress. I grabbed her hand, turning her back to me and pulling her close by the hip. That's better. Her ass not only was being hidden from others, but it also made my cock feel better. I was already hard, and I knew Harlow felt it. She moved her bottom against my hardness, and I helped her out to make it feel even better by pushing her into me.

My eyes stayed on her the whole time and I started to decide whether or not to stay or leave. Release sounded better than this torture. I knew Harlow was teasing and the thought of that made my cock twitch.

I leaned down, pressing a kiss to the side of her neck and licking a trail up to her ear. "I want to take you up to that room and fuck you," I whispered. She shivered and I heard her breath hitch. Good, so she wanted the same.

She turned around, looking up at me with her lids lowered and desire flashing in her eyes. "Okay," was all she said and from that moment on, all I saw was her naked in bed with her legs spread wide open ready for me to taste her.

CHAPTER THIRTY-ONE

Hunter

"Naked, love. I want you naked." The second we stepped into the bedroom, her dress was off and thrown to the floor with no care and her bra followed right behind. Harlow laid back on the bed, holding herself up on her elbows and looking at me with big, lustful eyes. My eyes fell to her breasts, perfectly displayed for me.

I slowly took off my shirt first, then my jeans, keeping on only my boxers. She was watching me but seemed a bit tense. "What's wrong?" I asked, standing by the end of the bed and looking down at her beauty. She shrugged, then licked her lips slowly.

"I'm just getting impatient. I want you inside me." Her words not only surprised me but also herself. Harlow never really said much when we were having sex. She let me do the talking and I knew she enjoyed it a little too much. But this time, she was straight forward, and it turned me on even

159

more.

I let a grin appear on my face and I slowly pushed down my boxers to let my cock free. I was aching already, needing to get inside her as quick as possible. But I wanted to see what else she would beg me for if I kept this at a slow pace.

"Is that so?" I asked in a low voice. The head of my cock was visible now that I let my boxers down some inches more.

She nodded, letting her frustration show on her face.

"Tell me again," I ordered. Her lips parted slightly, and her eyes took in the sight of my half-covered dick.

"Hunter, please," she whispered, almost breathless. I raised an eyebrow, letting her know that I wasn't playing around. I meant what I said, and I wanted her to listen.

"Tell me," I repeated.

This time, she licked her lips again and her eyes met mine again. "I want you to fuck me."

Her voice was so damn innocent and my cock jerked at her words. Fucking hell. That was enough to stop my teasing. I took off my briefs quickly, then reached for her panties and ripped them off her legs. A surprised sound came from her and when I looked back into her eyes, I slammed into her, making her scream out my name.

I quickly adjusted, pushing her up the bed so I could kneel between her spread legs and thrust into her harder. With every move, Harlow cried out and her hands gripped my shoulders tightly.

"Fuck, you're so tight. That tight pussy is mine,"

I said through gritted teeth and while one of my hands kept my body hovering over her, my other wrapped itself around Harlow's neck, lightly squeezing to make it feel good. I knew she liked that. She told me once and since then I would try my best not to hurt her. I tended to get a little rough when it came to fucking Harlow, but she'd always tell me to slow down or stop something as soon as it became a little too much to handle for her.

"Oh, God," she moaned, and I couldn't help but grin. "Told you before, love. Hunter's just fine."

She let out a laugh, slapping my shoulder and shaking her head. "You're such an idiot—oh, Hunter!" Her cries were getting louder and I wondered if the people in the rooms around us could hear her. But then, everyone was probably still outside at the party. The music was still playing but inside the room, I couldn't hear it that well. I was focusing on Harlow anyway.

I could tell she was close. She was squeezing my dick tightly, pulsating around me. The shaking of her body was also a sign of her wanting some release. But I wasn't done yet and I was, for once, being selfish. Sure, I wanted to make her come and feel good, but at the moment, pumping into her like a maniac was what I wanted just a little longer. I felt my cock throb and I had to hold it back.

"Turn," I simply said and pulled her left leg over to the other side, so she wasn't lying on her back anymore. I could now see her ass from the side, and I didn't hesitate to give it a slap before continuing to push into her hard and fast. Harlow turned her head into the pillow, crying out louder and repeating my name repeatedly.

"You like it rough, hm? My sweetheart likes it when I fuck her hard." Harlow just nodded as a response and I could tell she was trying to squeeze me tighter.

"Hunter, please," she begged, reaching up with her left hand to get a handful of my hair. She pulled me down and I kissed her, letting my tongue push through her lips and into her mouth. She returned the kiss, not having any problems with breathing.

Sweat was dripping down my forehead and even if the people outside could hear us, I wished I had opened up the window to let in some air. We didn't mind the cold. We're used to it from Hastings, and I knew Harlow adored the rain. She also enjoyed thunders and stormy nights. Those were her favorites. I often woke up with her wide awake in my arms, just looking out the window and observing the weather outside. It was adorable to watch her enjoy the little things in life.

"I'm gonna come." Her voice cracked and I needed to hurry up. I was keeping her from coming, but I wanted to come at the same time as her. I slowed down a bit but kept my thrusts hard.

"Fuck!" I growled and gripped her ass tightly with one hand while the other cupped the side of her face, making her look up at me.

The orgasm hit us both hard, making her shake and shiver and pressing her legs together. That only made it feel better and I stopped moving, coming inside of her and feeling her wet heat around me.

"Oh, my God," Harlow murmured as she came down from her high. I stayed inside of her, lowering my head to kiss her cheek before pressing my lips against hers.

"I love you so fucking much," I mumbled and didn't expect a response, since I already knew what it was.

CHAPTER THIRTY-TWO

Harlow

We were both lost in what we were doing that we forgot one important thing. Protection. Before he pushed into me, I did think about it for a second, but then I thought Hunter would probably remember to pull out. We had sex without a condom before when I got on birth control, but I had to stop taking that specific pill because I got major chest problems and headaches as side effects. I asked my gynecologist if that was normal and she told me that some girls needed to test different pills before they found the one that wouldn't be problematic. Since I couldn't just start taking several pills at once, I had to take breaks each month before trying a new one. And this month, I was taking that break. The last brand of pills I tried wasn't doing my body any justice either. I felt sick several hours after taking it and I puked, getting it out again. And the other thing was, by taking just one pill, you wouldn't be protected from getting pregnant. We knew that, though.

I wasn't sure how to tell Hunter. He wasn't really keeping up with my pill problem and I was now feeling a little guilty not talking about it. I should've remembered not being on the pill. Yet, I remember telling him about the new pill I was going to take a week ago.

It was all a little confusing and I was already overthinking everything and trying to talk myself into believing what I thought was right. Frankly, I had no idea why I was trying so hard when I knew exactly when the last time was that I took a pill and I knew for a fact that I was not on birth control.

"Can't sleep?" Hunter asked as he pulled me tighter against his chest, keeping his eyes closed and pressing his hand to my lower back to make sure I wasn't going anywhere. I looked up at him, studying his face to make sure he was awake and not just talking in his sleep.

"It's just a little warm in here." That was not an excuse since it really was hot in the room. "Mind if I open the window a bit?" I asked, kissing his jaw softly. He shook his head, letting his arms fall open for me to get up. I walked over to the big window and opened it, letting in some fresh air. I felt soreness between my legs, and I knew it was from Hunter slamming into me with a force that wasn't just making it hurt down there afterward, but also feel very good throughout.

"Something's on your mind," he mumbled as I climbed back into bed. He was now laying on his back, looking up at me as I sat there next to him and pulled the cover over my legs. I smiled at him, cupping his cheek in my hand and running my thumb over his stubbles.

"I was just remembering our night. It was perfect." I lied about what I was thinking of, but what I said was fully true.

He watched me closely for a while before running his fingers along my thigh. "Are you sore?"

I nodded, taking his hand in mine and lifting it to my mouth to kiss the back of it. "But I can handle it," I whispered and then cuddled up to him.

He pulled the cover up to our hips and put his arms around me again. "Of course, you can. You can handle anything." He stopped but I knew he was going to say more. These were his sentimental moments where he just spoke from deep inside of him, letting me know all his thoughts. "You're like…Superman. But, like, a girl. Supergirl," he said slowly, and I couldn't help but grin. I didn't say anything, knowing he had more to say. I loved listening to his thoughts.

"You've been through so much and you're still here. You're strong and your mind is incredible. You fascinate me each day with what you do and say," he said, his voice a little hoarse from sleep and probably also the humidity in this room. I smiled, lifting my hand again to play with his hair at the back of his head.

"Do you even realize what you've been through? Most people would break from shit like that but you…" He let his eyes wander all over my face before a smile spread on his lips. "You just grow from it all and you just turn into this incredibly kind and wonderful woman with each thing that comes at you with a force most people couldn't handle."

This time, he took my breath away. God, how did I even deserve him? With all the negativity surrounding us at the moment, Hunter was all I needed to make it all better. He often told me how perfect I was and how I'd inspire him to be a better person, but what he didn't know was, that he was the one helping me through the hard times. And he had no idea just how much I felt the same way about him.

I wanted to say something next, but I couldn't form words. Instead, I pushed myself up and steadied myself to hold my upper body up, then leaned down to kiss him passionately. I felt his smile get bigger, then he returned my kiss, cupping the back of my head. "I love you," I murmured, wanting everything that was happening around us with Dean to just end and disappear from our lives. This wasn't just about me or Jagger. Hunter got dragged into it all because of me and I hated the thought of him having to be careful whenever he went outside.

"And I love you. So fucking much." He broke the kiss to look at me again and the wrinkling of his nose told me he wasn't happy about something. "I'm turning into some corny idiot because of you."

I laughed this time, shaking my head at him. "I like it. I like it when you talk to me and open up. Your mind is an incredibly interesting place, Hunter. I'd love to hear more of your thoughts."

"I think you'll get to hear more of them in the future," he said, then his expression turned serious. "I want to get better. For you. I want to clean up my mind. Become a better man," he whispered.

To me, he couldn't get any better than that. But I knew what he meant. He was still struggling with his mental health, even though he went to a psychologist a few weeks back. He said it didn't really work for him, or that he needed a new one, but since then, he never actually looked for another one.

I was thinking about asking him about it, or what his plans were about therapy. I just noticed that each time he opened up to me, something about him slightly changed and I started to think that I was his therapy.

CHAPTER THIRTY-THREE

Hunter

We arrived back in Hastings around noon and Harlow was being quieter than usual. At first, I thought she was just tired from our night in Sutton, but something was on her mind. I stepped inside the house after her and put the duffel bag down.

"All right," I said. "Talk to me." Harlow turned, surprised by my demanding voice. Her brows were pulled tight and the look on her face told me she was hiding something.

"About what?" she asked, trying to sound innocent.

"You got something on your mind. I need to know what it is, or I won't stop asking. Now, go ahead. Talk." She seemed worried, yet, I wouldn't back down.

She lowered her head and picked the skin on her thumbs nervously. She didn't look back up and she wasn't about to talk, either.

"Harlow," I said in a low voice. I didn't want to

scare her, but I needed to get whatever was inside her mind out of there. "I've told you before. You can tell me anything."

"I know," she responded quickly, now looking up at me with a sad smile. Her eyes were filled with unshed tears and I suddenly felt pain in my chest. I hated seeing her cry and not knowing what was wrong made it ten times worse.

I stepped closer to grab her hands and hold them tightly in mine. "Did I do something wrong?" I was whispering now, and my body was tense. She quickly shook her head, which eased the tension a little. "Then what is it? Talk to me, Harlow."

She sighed, not taking her eyes off mine and letting the tears roll down her face. "I'm not on birth control," she whispered, and I had to let that sentence go through my mind once more before realizing what she said.

We had unprotected sex. And I came inside of her. I repeated those words over and over before running my hand through my hair and looking down at her stomach. "You told me you were on the pill." And she did. I know she told me. Why would I not worry about protection otherwise?

"You told me you were taking another pill. Why did you stop taking them?" My voice was getting louder and I was about to lose control.

There are other ways to talk about this, man.

"I forgot," she sobbed and covered her face with her hands. "I'm sorry, I forgot." It seemed almost as if she was protecting herself from me. She saw my anger building up on my face and that terrified her. She saw the worst of me when I got angry. Not this

170

time. She didn't deserve it.

I took a deep breath, trying to calm myself and remember that we couldn't turn back time anyway. So, what happened, happened. Besides, I was already overthinking it all. Thinking too much about something I wasn't a hundred percent sure of.

I reached for her hands to be able to see her face and luckily, she let me hold her hands in mine. I studied her for a while, then decided I was ready to talk normally without getting angry again.

"It will be okay. I mean, it doesn't mean you're…" The next word didn't sound right, so I just let it go. She knew what I meant. Just thinking about it was making me sick. Not that I wouldn't want to have her baby, but…the time just wasn't right. At all.

"You can do a test, right? We'll get you one. And…whatever the result is," I took a deep breath, then sighed, "we'll decide from there, okay?"

I sounded like an asshole. She was obviously feeling bad for not telling me and I was just making it worse by my stupid try to make this a positive situation. What a dick I am.

Harlow nodded, letting her head down again. "I'm sorry," she repeated.

I shook my head, lifting her chin so she would look at me again. "We're in this together, sweetheart. Hell, this is life. Shit like this happens all the time and people still manage to go through life."

She stared at me with big eyes. Shit. I said something to make it worse again. "Shit like this," she repeated, furrowing her brows.

A groan escaped me and I decided in that very moment that I was indeed a huge fucking asshole. "I'm sorry. I'm being insensitive about this," I told her in all honesty.

"You wouldn't want my baby," she said, her sentence sounding more like a fact than a question. I quickly shook my head.

"Fuck, of course I want your baby. Hell, I want ten if they're yours, but life right now is fucking insane, Harlow. Your father is going crazy out there, I still work for Gunner, and I'm still battling with my damn mind. You being pregnant would be dangerous. But if any of those things I just listed wouldn't be problems you and I must deal with right now, then, hell yeah, I'd be ready for a little girl running around, looking just as pretty as her momma."

Again, it felt like I was talking nonsense. I was just letting my mind and mouth run out and I hoped it somehow made at least a little sense. Harlow was studying me, letting me know she was unsure of what I just said too.

"You're right," she whispered. Her arms came up and wrapped around my neck while her body pressed into mine. I waited for her to say more, but instead of talking, her lips touched mine and I immediately returned the kiss.

"I think we're overreacting," she said after leaning back to look into my eyes. I nodded slowly, holding her close to me with my hands on her lower back. "But we need to buy a pregnancy test," she added.

"I'll text Bliss. She probably has one laying

around at home," I said, wishing I didn't have that much information about my sister.

Harlow bit back a smile. "Why's that?" she asked. I shrugged and let out a deep sigh. "Don't know. You can ask her when she's here."

"Hmm," she replied, sounding interested in my sister's pregnancy test storage at her apartment. "I'll make us something to eat." She gave me one more kiss before walking over to the kitchen.

I pulled out my phone and opened up Bliss's chat. I reread my last text about talking about her and Jagger, and I decided, today was a good day to do so. Harlow could listen too. In the end, her brother was part of it all just like my sister.

Hunter: Do me a favor?

Bliss: Depends

Hunter: Bring a pregnancy test over.

Bliss: Why lol OMG HUNTER YOU DID NOT

Hunter: Christ, relax.

Bliss: Hunter…

Hunter: Just get over here, Bliss. Please.

CHAPTER THIRTY-FOUR

Bliss

Having pregnancy tests around the apartment was normal. At least, for me it was. I did have protected sex, but I got paranoid as soon as my period didn't come as expected. So, those little sticks filled a whole drawer in my bathroom. I also didn't trust many guys I slept with. I just had them over for fun or to let out some frustration. In the last few weeks, though, only one guy came over regularly, and I was hoping not to see him when I arrived at his house.

Hunter told me to bring a test for Harlow. They were probably overreacting, or Harlow was being paranoid herself. Yet, all I was thinking about was Jagger. The truth was; the thing between Jagger and I started way before Hunter started dating Harlow. We kept it on the down-low, not wanting either of them to find out and make things weird, but since they went for it right in front of our eyes, showing us their true love for each other, Jagger wanted to let especially Hunter know, that he could do just the same. Fuck his sister.

That was the difference. Hunter and Harlow made love, while Jagger and I just fucked. That's what he told me each time he came around, wanting to escape his sister's new relationship.

He told me many times about the way he felt about it. He was angry at first. Very angry, letting it all out on me between the sheets. He acted like a crazed man and I, like a good fuckbuddy, just went with it and let him fuck me as hard as he wanted to.

Jagger also cried in front of me, wondering if Harlow loved him less, now that she had another guy in her life. I let him understand that Harlow's love for him was so much different than for Hunter. Jagger was Harlow's hero, protecting her since she was born and every time she looked at him, I knew there was no love greater than her love for him.

After telling him that, he calmed down. It felt good knowing that he listened. At least, when it came to his sister.

I realized I was sitting in my car in front of Jagger's house for several minutes before I saw the front door open out of the corner of my eyes. I turned my head, watching Hunter walk down the few steps. He had a concerned look on his face and I quickly stepped out of the car, smiling at him. Before I could say something, he spoke.

"You okay?" he asked, reaching me and eyeing me carefully.

I nodded. "Yes. I just remembered something I gotta do later tonight. How's Harlow?" I changed the subject and closed the car door.

"Fine, I think. Come on." We walked back to the house and the second I stepped inside Harlow came walking toward me with a genuine smile. That's what I adored about her. Her positive aura was incredibly contagious, and you couldn't help but feel just as happy as she was.

"Bliss," she exclaimed in her usual sweet voice and I hugged her tight, letting all the thoughts about Jagger fly away.

"Hi, darling. It's good to see you again," I told her and then backed up to look at her. Her smile never faded.

"It's good to see you too. I'm sorry if we bothered you."

I shook my head and sat down on the couch, lifting my handbag up on my lap and getting out what Hunter asked me to bring. I looked back up at Harlow and smiled. "Don't worry about it. I wasn't busy. Here." I held the pregnancy test in her direction, and she took it slowly.

After studying it, she looked back at me. "How long does this take?" she asked.

"Just a couple of minutes," I explained, then gave her an encouraging smile. "It'll be okay, Low." And with that, she glanced at Hunter, then disappeared in the bathroom. I sighed, putting my bag down and leaning back on the couch.

"Was it last night?" I asked Hunter, who was still standing in the middle of the living room with his hands hidden in his pockets. His eyes shifted from the bathroom door to mine and his brows furrowed slightly.

"Yeah," he said slowly, not sure why I needed to

know that.

I lifted an eyebrow. "So, you do know that the test will come out negative, right?" I asked, wondering if he knew anything about a woman's body.

"And why's that?". Lord, he'd have been better off staying in school instead of becoming a criminal.

"Hunter, you two just had sex some hours ago. Women take pregnancy tests when their periods don't come, and for cases like this, there is the morning-after pill. So the sperm doesn't even get the chance to impregnate her."

It felt like I was his sex-ed teacher.

"And why doesn't Harlow know that?" he hissed, suddenly annoyed with me.

I rolled my eyes. "Because she's panicking and stressed."

"Great excuse," Hunter mumbled and ran a hand through his hair. Then, suddenly, relief came over him. "So, she's not pregnant."

"The test will come out negative, but that doesn't mean she's not pregnant. She'll have to take that morning after pill," I explained.

"I'm so stupid," I heard Harlow say from the hallway. She was looking at both of us, holding the unopened test in her hand. Hunter and I turned our heads to look at her. "God, I'm so stupid!" she repeated and covered her forehead with her hand. She must've heard our conversation since this house had thin walls.

"Why didn't I think about that? I have to go get that pill."

I couldn't help but chuckle. "Sorry I didn't tell you before."

Harlow waved her hand and sighed, sitting down on the armrest of Hunter's recliner. Hunter took her hand and kissed the back of it. "I wasn't thinking either, love. We'll just go to the pharmacy and get it later." Harlow nodded slowly, handing me the unused test. She was seemingly annoyed with herself. Hell, shit like that happened. No big deal. She'll get the pill and everything will be fine.

Jagger's voice coming from the front door calling Harlow's name sent shivers down my spine in a weird way. Why was I afraid of being in the same room as him and the other two? His footsteps came closer and I didn't turn to look his way. He was standing right there, yet I refused to turn and look.

"Did something happen?" he asked, breaking the silence. Hunter and Harlow shook their heads but kept their mouths shut. *Great support*, I thought.

"Feels like a damn funeral in here." He walked over to the kitchen, turning his back to me and I finally looked his way. His clothes were dirty from the cars he worked on and the white cap he was wearing had black fingerprints all over it. "How was the trip?" he asked, now turning with a beer in his hand. His eyes met mine for a split second before he looked at Harlow.

"Perfect. It was amazing," she told him with a smile, then wrapped her arm around Hunter's shoulders. "Hunter got me my favorite R.E.M. LP."

Jagger sat down next to me, which surprised me. He was acting weird. The last time I saw him he was all over me.

"So now you can listen to it on your new record player." He grinned, and Harlow nodded excitedly.

I had enough of him already. I hated him for the way he acted around others when I was around. It was almost as if I only existed when we were alone. I took in a deep breath, standing up from the couch and grabbing my bag. "I should go. I'll see you guys around," I directed to Hunter and Harlow. They both just nodded, feeling just as awkward as I did.

I gave them a tight smile before heading for the door. I didn't say another word, mainly just to let Jagger know how pissed I was thanks to him.

When I opened the door, Jagger's hand wrapped around my wrist and he pulled me back just enough for me to stop in my tracks.

"You okay?" he asked, and I almost laughed.

"Why do you care?"

He sighed, pulling at my wrist to make me turn to him. I did, so he would see my expression. "Don't start this bullshit, Bliss. I'm tired. Work was shit and all I need is sleep. Now, tell me. Is everything okay?"

Damn him. He could ignore me all he wanted, but in the end, I was the one running back to him like a fool.

I slowly nodded. "I'm fine," I whispered, pulling my wrist free from his grasp. He studied me for a while and nodded slowly.

"Mind if I come over tonight?" Yes. I did mind. Because all he wanted was to let out his frustration and make me feel like a piece of shit in the end. But of course, this was Jagger. So, rejecting him wasn't in my schedule, ever.

I shook my head and even offered him a time. How stupid was I? "Nine?" I asked, and he smiled, leaning in to kiss me as a confirmation that nine was perfect and he would once again come over to fuck me, then leave in the middle of the night.

CHAPTER THIRTY-FIVE

Harlow

Hunter witnessed me taking the morning after pill at the pharmacy and his face was immediately filled with relief. It was obvious he didn't want to become a dad right now and to be fully honest, I wasn't ready to get pregnant. Just like Hunter said, it wasn't the right time.

We went to go get the pill right after Bliss left. Jagger looked emotionless as he came back into the living room and I wondered what he said to her. It felt like whatever they had going on wasn't making either of them happy, but asking Jagger about it seemed not to be right at the moment. He looked stressed out because of Bliss and Bliss looked hurt. Hunter told me to just let them live before we pushed ourselves into their private business.

Before driving back home, Hunter took me to the record store he told me about yesterday and I bought myself five new records. All of them were used, but still in perfect condition. Before we left

181

the store, Hunter got a call from Jagger and the look on his face was enough for me to understand that he had to go to work. For Gunner, of course.

We arrived back home but instead of getting out of the car, I turned to look at Hunter.

"Will I ever get to meet Gunner?" I asked, immediately regretting the question. Hunter let out a harsh laugh, shaking his head.

"Fuck, no."

Saw that one coming, I thought. Without another word, Hunter got out of the car and walked around the back of it and over to my side. He opened the door for me, and I stepped out, grabbing the bag with my new records in it. "And you're really sure you're okay with Bennett *babysitting* me until you're back?" Jagger arranged Bennett to look after me while they went to work. When Hunter told me about it, he looked pissed. Almost furious, to say the least.

"I'd beat the shit out of him if I had a say in this. But your brother thinks you'll be safe with him, so I'll just accept it and move on and try not to get angry because I'm a grown man." He stopped for a second, then added: "As long as you're safe, I don't mind another man looking after you."

I couldn't help but laugh. He was being incredibly sweet lately, showing me how much he wanted to change. He'd come a long way already, so a little jealousy was okay with me.

"He's doing his job. I don't think he wants to lose it by trying to get in a client's panties." I grinned, looking up at him.

He shrugged, then took my hand in his. "But if

he tries to, I'll make sure he'll be the next man I kill after tonight's guy."

Knowing that he and my brother killed people for money didn't bother me as much as it should've. Probably because no matter what I said, they wouldn't just stop doing it, and the other thing was, I saw past the crimes they were committing. I loved both of them unconditionally. Like Bonnie supported Clyde through all the bad he did. In my case, though, I didn't help Hunter do the criminal stuff.

I tried not to think much about the fact that I was the Bonnie to Hunter's Clyde. Funnily enough, Bonnie Parker was also born on October 1st.

When we reached the front door, Bennett's car pulled up behind Hunter's and he got out, wearing a white Oxford shirt and black pants.

"The fuck did he dress up for?" Hunter mumbled next to me and I slapped his chest.

"Be nice," I whispered, stepping aside as Jagger came out the door just in time.

"We should be home by midnight. Just stay until we get back," Jagger said to Bennett as he made his way up the steps to our door. Bennett nodded, looking at Jagger and Hunter, then at me. A smile spread on his face and just then I realized he was holding a bag in his left hand.

"I got us some dinner. Thought I couldn't just come to hang out here without bringing something."

I heard Hunter mumble something behind me, but I ignored it, smiling back at Bennett. "That's nice of you, thank you."

Bennett then gazed back up at the two men standing behind me and nodded once. "You guys gonna be okay? Gunner all right?" he asked, sounding more serious now.

"Yeah, we'll manage," Jagger answered and then kissed the top of my head. "See you later, sweet girl."

I looked up at him and nodded. "Be careful," I warned both of them and then Hunter cupped my face in his hands and pressed a kiss to my lips, probably just to remind Bennett of the fact that he was my boyfriend.

I returned the kiss, hoping it wasn't too awkward for the others to just stand there and watch, but then, I wanted Hunter's kisses, so I enjoyed them.

"I love you," he whispered against my lips and I pulled back to look into his eyes.

"I love you too. Now, go. We'll be fine." Hunter nodded, then gave Bennett one last look before leaving with Jagger.

I entered the house, Bennett following behind closely. That's when it hit me. Bennett knew about them being hitmen. But why was he so casual about it? He was working for the law, not against it. So why was he letting Jagger and Hunter still go and kill people?

"Everything okay?" he asked and walked to the kitchen to put down his bag. I nodded slowly, then watched him take out some vegetables and two steaks. Oh, so he was going to cook.

"I was just wondering…" I started saying, then stopped myself because I reminded myself about Hunter's words. Gunner's none of my business. But then, I already knew enough.

"You're like a cop, right? I mean, you could easily just arrest people." Bennett nodded, then a grin appeared on his face. "And now you're wondering why I know about your brother and your boyfriend's illegal work and don't do anything about it?"

Yes. That. I nodded slowly and studied his face. He chuckled and opened the fridge. "Because I know Gunner. Even if he's got some illegal business going on, his men, like your brother and Hunter, they take down people who've done bad things. Sure, hitmen aren't really good people either, but why would I arrest people who make sure others won't rape or abuse children anymore? Or, rob banks or innocent families?"

Oh, okay. Well, now I have a whole new picture painted in my head. I just nodded again, not really wanting to hear any more of those things. I'd been abused by my father and knowing other kids had to go through something like that as well just hurt.

"I didn't mean to upset you," he said.

"You didn't. Thanks for telling me, I guess." Bennett nodded and closed the fridge again after putting his groceries inside.

"No worries. You want a little update on your father?" he then asked, and I wasn't sure I wanted to. But then, the more I knew, the more I would feel safe, I thought.

"Okay," I told him and set down on the couch, the records still in the bag and on my lap. He walked back to the living room and sat down across from me. "My partner's watching him. Dean's got his car parked in a parking lot in front of a laundromat. He's been sitting in his car the whole time, staring straight ahead. He's exhausted, I think. Not sure he'll keep up with this shit any longer than two days."

I wasn't sure what to think about that. I hated Dean for what he did in the past and what he was doing now. Yet, I wanted him to get better. He was obviously not in his right mind. But then, there was not much I could do.

I took a deep breath, nodding slowly and giving Bennett a smile. "Would you like to listen to my new records?" I asked, trying to change the mood. I reached into the bag and pulled out one of the five records, revealing an old Oasis album.

He looked a little surprised. "You still listen to vinyl?" he asked with a bright smile. I nodded, then got up and walked over to the new record player Jagger got me.

"Music sounds better this way," I explained. He chuckled and leaned back.

"Can't say you're wrong about that."

Turned out, spending an evening with an investigator wasn't as bad as I thought.

CHAPTER THIRTY-SIX

Harlow

Bennett's cooking wasn't as good as Hunter's. I did enjoy it, but Hunter clearly knew a lot more about what he was doing in the kitchen than Bennett. While he was cooking, I took a shower and then cleaned up around the house a little. After dinner, I helped him with the dishes and then we decided to watch a movie.

I didn't understand why Hunter was jealous of him. Sure, Bennett was a good looking guy, but he wasn't trying anything on me. He was just being nice and looking after me. Also, I was pretty sure about him having a girlfriend. He got a few messages from someone with the name Ellis and next to the name there was a heart. Another reason why I felt comfortable around him.

We didn't talk much, but when we did, it all came easy and didn't feel forced at all. And as time went by, I felt tiredness come over me and I was ready to go to bed. It was past eleven, and Jagger said they would be back around midnight, yet I wasn't sure I could stay awake until they were home. So, I closed my eyes and didn't mind the fact that I was about to fall asleep on the couch.

I felt my body relax and I knew I was going to be out in some minutes but when Bennett's phone rang, I was suddenly wide awake, and I sat up again to look at him. He took the call and kept his eyes on the TV.

"Drew, what's new?" Bennett asked his partner. Having a job like theirs must be boring. Just sitting in their car and observing someone for hours sounded dull to me. But then, they probably also had other tasks to do.

"Are you sure?" Bennett looked at me, slightly concerned. I straightened my back, knowing they were talking about something Dean-related.

"All right. Keep an eye on him. I'll be right there." He hung up and got up from the couch, tapping on his phone. "You need to stay here. I'll lock you in so nothing's gonna happen. I'll call Jagger to let him know you'll be home alone."

I didn't understand what he was trying to achieve at that moment, so I gave him a confused look and got up as well. "What is going on?" I asked, watching him lift his phone to his ear. He then looked at me and his serious expression told me that he didn't have much time to discuss it with me.

"Dean is at Frankie's Diner and he's about to go inside." I furrowed my brows, wondering why Dean was at my workplace when he probably knew I wasn't there.

"Jagger," Bennett said into the phone, his eyes

on mine again. "We got a situation with Dean at Frankie's. Drew's watching him but Dean's about to walk inside. I'm headed over there." He paused and listened to what Jagger was saying, then nodded. "All right, I'll take her with me and meet you guys there. Hurry." He once again hung up the phone and sighed, shaking his head in disagreement.

"It's not safe for you there, but your brother wants you there so Hunter can take you to his place while we handle Dean."

I nodded, in my mind thanking my brother for his great idea not to let me here all alone.

***

Hunter

That son of a bitch was lucky Harlow and I weren't working tonight, or else I was sure I couldn't keep from hurting him. He crossed the line once by following us around like a mad man. And he crossed it twice, now that he was walking into the diner with his dirty clothes on. Jagger and I arrived at the diner just five minutes after Bennett had called. Luckily, we were just driving back home, and I had informed Frankie about Dean. They knew each other personally; both grew up here in Hastings. I told Frankie to be careful, since Dean probably had a gun on him, but Frankie just laughed it off and shot back with: "I got one too."

We were now standing behind our parked cars with Drew, Bennett's partner, and Jagger was looking through Drew's binoculars to get a better view of what was happening inside.

"I'm gonna kill that motherfucker," he mumbled, and the tension could be seen all over his body. He was angry and ready to burst, but he couldn't do that until Harlow got here with Bennett and I would take her home with me. Harlow didn't need to see whatever was going to happen.

"Easy, brother. Dean looks lost. Probably outta his mind," I told him. I heard a car drive up next to us and I turned to see Harlow get out with fear in her eyes. I met her halfway and pulled her into my arms. "Hey, sweetheart," I whispered, holding her close to my body. She didn't say a word, instead, she hugged me tighter, letting me know that she was scared.

"It's okay. They'll take care of him. I'll take you home where you're safe." Harlow shook her head at my plan and backed up so she could get a glimpse of the diner.

"Frankie is in there," she said and gazed up at Jagger. "He needs to get out of there. Everyone needs to get out of there!" Her voice grew louder, and I could tell by the shaking in her voice that she was about to cry.

"We got it under control, Low. Go home with Hunter," Jagger told her and kept his eyes on Dean.

"Shit," Drew mumbled while keeping the binoculars he was now looking through directed on the diner.

"We gotta get in there. He's got a gun," he added and then looked at Bennett with a nod.

"Take her home!" Jagger roared at me and I

grabbed Harlow's wrist to pull her to my car. She didn't move and tried to free herself from my grip.

"Harlow, get in the fucking car," I said in a calm but harsh voice which didn't seem to bother her at all. She kept on struggling and tried to get my hand off her with her free hand.

"Hunter, now!" Jagger shouted, and just like Bennett and Drew, he grabbed his gun and unlocked it so he was ready to shoot if necessary.

"Harlow," I warned again but she kept on resisting, tears now rolling down her face.

"I can't just leave!" she argued, and I was about to lose my patience. Bennett and Drew were already walking up to the diner and Jagger turned to us, wrapping his hand around Harlow's neck so she had to look up at him. He looked mad and I was damn close to telling him not to lay a hand on her like that. But then, Harlow was being stubborn in a dangerous situation and I wasn't having it, just like Jagger.

"I got this under control, goddammit! You need to listen to me and go with Hunter." His words were full of anger and I knew he wasn't just about to get Dean arrested. Jagger had other things in mind.

"I can't leave!" Harlow was clearly shocked by the way her brother was treating her at that very moment, but she wasn't letting loose. She wanted to stay. And just as I expected, she would witness bad things if she'd stay.

Chapter Thirty-Seven

Harlow

I winced at the sound of a gun being fired. Jagger's grip around my neck immediately loosened and he and Hunter quickly stepped in front of me. I heard shouting and screaming coming from the diner and even without seeing what was really happening, I knew it was chaos.

"Stay with her," Jagger ordered Hunter, and then he ran toward the diner, where people were running out from the door. Luckily, not many people were inside, but the ones who were able to escape the dramatic scene on the inside.

"Get in the car," Hunter told me, now his voice sounding even harder than before. I couldn't move, even though I was trying to. I couldn't keep my eyes off Dean, who was standing in the middle of the diner, his left arm around Nixon's neck holding him locked beside him, and his other hand pointing his gun right against Nixon's temple, ready to shoot an innocent young man.

The sight of that was terrifying and seeing Jagger walk in on that scene was making me feel sick to my stomach. I saw Bennet and Drew standing some feet away from Dean, holding their guns in his direction and it looked like they were talking to him calmly. But the two of them didn't matter to Dean since his eyes were fixed on Jagger, who stepped next to Drew, his gun in his hand next to his side.

"Harlow," I heard Hunter's voice in the distance, and I shook off his hands from my shoulders. I wasn't going to listen. What I was seeing was making my heart race faster than ever and the pain pulling my chest together was a sign of fear I was feeling.

Yet, I couldn't look away.

***

Hunter

The first gunshot hit a lamp on the ceiling, which caused the lightbulb to break. Dean clearly didn't think this through, since he was holding an innocent man as some kind of hostage right in front of everyone. I knew Bennett and Drew were wearing bulletproof vests underneath, but Jagger didn't, and I was scared that idiot was going to get hurt, or worse, killed by his own fucking father right in front of his sister's eyes.

I knew Jagger wanted revenge, but this wasn't going to end well. Dean was crazy and he wasn't afraid to use that gun. He wasn't thinking straight and knowing his son was standing right there, he might as well just take a chance.

They were talking, Dean still holding poor Nixon in his headlock with a gun to his head. Bennett and Drew kept their guns on Dean, and I knew that if Dean was going to shoot Nixon, or anyone else, they'd shoot back with no hesitation.

That's when I saw someone move in the back, slowly walking toward Dean. Frankie. He was sneaking up on him and that was the biggest mistake he could've made.

"Shit," I mumbled and grabbed Harlow's hand, ready to open the car door and push her inside. She didn't need to see all that.

But I was too late. As Frankie stepped closer to Dean and reached for his gun, Dean let go of Nixon, making him hit the floor hard. Dean then turned to fight Frankie off, holding his gun tightly in his hand. It all happened too fast and suddenly, another gunshot rang through my ears and Harlow let out a loud cry, calling Frankie's name.

That's when I saw Frankie drop to the floor with blood coming out of his chest.

"No!" Harlow cried out, and the way her body shook made my heart ache terribly. As sad as it was, I couldn't just stand there and watch it all go down in misery. I had to help, or else more people would get hurt. So, I swung open the door of my car and grabbed Harlow by the shoulders, pushing her inside.

"This will be over soon," I assured her, and before she could fight back, I locked her in and ran toward the diner, making my way to the back entrance. I could hear Harlow scream from inside the car but I couldn't let another man get shot in there unless it was Dean himself.

So I ignored the pain that was growing inside my chest and turned into the cold-blooded killer who killed people who caused bad things in the world. I needed Dean to be gone. Out of Harlow's life and out of Jagger's too.

When I entered through the back, I could finally hear what was really going on. I heard Nixon cry, asking his uncle to wake up and telling him that everything will be all right soon. I didn't think so, seeing that bullet go right through Frankie's chest.

"Who's next, huh?" Dean growled, and I finally reached the front, stopping right by the kitchen where I could see them all. Jagger's eyes were on Dean's, not taking them off of him. He wanted more to happen. He was ready to fight but I wouldn't let it get that far. Harlow needed him. Hell, I needed him. So, my goal was to stop Dean's gun from going off again.

"Let's put the gun down, Dean. You've done enough damage already," Bennett said, sounding too damn calm for my liking. Did he really think he could make this all better by asking Dean to put down his gun? Jesus Christ.

Why isn't Bennett shooting him already? But then, having Dean suffer for the rest of his life and rot in prison sounded more appealing than having him killed instantly.

Dean shook his head at Bennett, turning his head to look at Jagger. A slow grin appeared on Dean's face while he raised his gun, pointing it directly at Jagger. *Fucking hell, just shoot him already!*

"Don't you have anything to say to your good ol' dad, son?" Dean slurred his words and I was suddenly unsure as to why I was just standing there, not helping out. Jagger's eyes were filled with unshed tears and the trembling of his bottom lip was a sign of sadness suddenly developing inside of him.

"Speechless, huh?" Dean chuckled and then clenched his jaw, his hand holding the gun starting to shake. "Always knew you're a fucking weak piece of shit. You've never spoken up to me and always ran like a scared little shit. Why don't you show me how fucking tough you are now! Show me that you've grown some balls in all these years!" Dean's voice was loud, and I saw Jagger hurting from his father's words. Jagger knew whatever he was saying wasn't true. He was strong. Made sure his little sister was safe and he cared for her more than he cared about his own damn life.

"FUCKING TALK TO ME!" Dean roared, and I saw Jagger wince, almost as if he were scared of his father. But he kept quiet and stared at Dean. "That's what I thought." Dean laughed and shook his head.

"Not even one word. I came here just to see you and that little cunt and all I fucking get is fucking silence," he exclaimed in an almost humorous tone. That's when it was over for Jagger. He wasn't taking anymore of Dean's bullshit. And thank fuck, I was waiting on that moment.

With one quick lift of his gun, Jagger pointed it directly at his father, his finger on the trigger and ready to pull. "Rest easy, Pa," Jagger whispered, pulling the trigger with no mercy.

EPILOGUE

October 3rd, 3:37 AM

Harlow

On the night of Dean's death, October 3rd, Jagger and I couldn't stop holding each other. On the couch, I cuddled up to him and he wrapped his arms around me tight, kissing my forehead over and over again. We sat there in silence and we both let out all of the tension that had built up through all those years, thanks to our father, who didn't take his role as a leading and protecting figure as serious as he should've.

Hunter was sitting there on the recliner, his elbows propped up on his knees and his hands rubbing against each other from time to time. His eyes stayed mainly on the small table in front of us but he wasn't talking either. It was late, but I knew he wasn't going to leave until he was sure that he could leave the two of us alone. I didn't want him to leave. He was part of me and I felt just as safe around him as Jagger.

I knew Hunter only wanted to protect me back at the diner by locking me inside his car, but from where I was sitting, I had the perfect view of my brother killing Dean. It wasn't the bullet burying itself through Dean's head that made me scream, but Jagger's face filled with anger and fear that I worried about the most. I saw the hurt in his eyes from the distance and I knew that very moment would change his life forever.

It wasn't easy growing up with an abusive father and then having to take care of a younger sibling from a very young age, but Jagger lived through hell and he made it out alive, saving me too. My love couldn't grow any bigger for him and all I wished for was that Jagger to not have any regrets after what happened some hours ago.

We were lucky the cops weren't involved in that drama. Bennet and Drew promised us to take care of the situation and get rid of Dean's body so no one would think he was killed by someone. I didn't want to know any more details about how they would get rid of his body. All I really cared about was Frankie. He was innocent, yet he was the victim of a brutal murder, caused by someone crazy enough to shoot a man who had no bad intentions.

Frankie was a great man. He cared about me and treated me like a daughter. He supported my choices about school and work, even if they weren't the right ones. He also grew on Hunter and Hunter started to grow on Frankie too. I thought about how it all could've been avoided. Frankie's death was worse than my own father's and I didn't' feel guilt at all.

Nixon was lost after Bennett and Drew covered both corpses with big sheets, so we wouldn't have to look at them anymore. I hugged Nixon tight, hoping he someday could forgive us for what happened to Frankie. Surprisingly enough, he hugged me back, crying into my shoulder. That's when I couldn't help my sobs from escaping.

Eventually, Drew drove Nixon home to his family and I made sure I had his phone number to reach him as soon as we knew more about his funeral. I wanted to be there. For Frankie.

The thought of Dean's funeral didn't even cross my mind and that was okay. I just wanted them to get rid of him. I was done with him and I knew Jagger was too.

In all honesty, there was not much more to say about Dean. He didn't deserve it. It felt like a heavy weight was lifted from my shoulders and I could finally move on.

"It's over," Jagger whispered against my head, giving me one more kiss and running his hand through my hair. I opened my eyes to look up at him and nodded.

"It's over." I repeated his words with a smile that I wondered was even visible. I doubted it. But it felt good to say those words.

***

October 18th

Fifteen days had passed since Frankie was killed, and I visited his grave every day since his funeral ten days ago. It was a beautiful ceremony. Jagger, Hunter, and I got to meet Frankie's lovely family, and Nixon introduced us to his mother, who was Frankie's sister. One thing was bothering me, though. They all thought Frankie died from a heart attack. The bullet wound on his chest wasn't visible thanks to the suit he was wearing, and it covered up all the lies about his death.

I could see how hard it was for Nixon to not tell anyone about the true cause of Frankie's death, yet, he had to keep quiet.

I held Hunter and Jagger's hands throughout the whole ceremony, receiving all their strength and love.

Before we left, Nixon handed me a note with my name on it, signed by Frankie. "I found this while going through his stuff in his office. I didn't read it. There was one for me too." Nixon smiled and pulled me into his embrace. "Stay safe," he whispered, and I nodded.

"You too."

He stepped back and nodded once, looking at Hunter and Jagger before walking back to his mother, who was standing in front of Frankie's gravestone.

I still hadn't opened the note, but I was about to read it out loud in front of Jagger, Hunter, and Bliss. We were all sitting in our living room, Jagger on the recliner, Hunter next to me on one couch, and Bliss on the other.

I unfolded the note and started reading it.

Dear Low,

I know this seems a little too forward, but I also know that I would never be brave enough to say this to you. I'm not good with words, but I hope it's enough for you to understand what I'm trying to tell you. I was lucky enough to get to meet a strong and kind-hearted young woman like you and even if I'm not a father, I know that I would've wished for my daughter to be just like you. You've helped around the diner a lot and I hope you stay for many more years. If that is the case, I want you to have the diner. Take over. Make it the best diner in this goddamn town.

Now, I know it's a little much for me to ask from you, but you're the only one I want to keep my diner up for as long as possible. If you say no, then I guess I'll have to ask Nixon. (Please, don't let that happen.) And if you do say yes, then I also wouldn't mind for your wannabe badass boyfriend to help you out in the kitchen. Again, don't feel pressured. Take your time.

- Frankie

"Oh, wow," Bliss said in awe and I looked up at her with tears in my eyes.

"He probably wanted to give me this someday," I pointed out and looked over at Hunter. He was watching me closely.

"So, what do you think?" he asked, surprising me with his lighthearted tone.

"I…I don't know," I said in all honesty. "I mean, isn't that…" I stopped, wondering why I couldn't get myself to just take the offer and start all over again.

"What about Gunner?" I asked Hunter. He shrugged. "My contract with him is over. I would love to stay here with you. We could renovate the diner. Clean up a bit and start over."

That sounded nice. I didn't want to leave Hastings. Not yet. So, maybe taking over Frankie's diner wasn't a bad idea. I would be doing it for Frankie, in the end.

***

Hunter

January 17th

Life was good. Harlow made me move in with her after Jagger left Hastings. I had a long talk with him before he explained to Harlow why he wanted to leave town. He told me about the demons following him around. Even though he knew Dean was gone, he didn't feel like Hastings was the right place for him to heal from all the shit that happened. He needed a fresh start and wanted to get out of Hastings to clear his mind.

Jagger gave us his new address and told us to go visit him whenever we felt like seeing him, so I made sure we headed over to his new home once a week.

Harlow and I were busy with the diner. We renovated it slightly, making sure everything was running smoothly for the re-opening of Frankie's diner. Harlow kept the name and also made sure everyone remembered Frankie's the way it was with the first owner running it.

People still liked to eat at the diner, and I was able to hire some more cooks and waiters. I knew Frankie was struggling with paying his employees and that was why no one wanted to work for him, but since I didn't have anything better to do with my money, I made sure everyone got enough at the end of the month.

What was most important to me was Harlow's happiness. She didn't like the fact that Jagger wasn't close anymore, but they called and texted almost daily. Bliss was also still around, still working at the diner on the highway and visiting us as much as possible. She barely talked about Jagger and I wondered if they were still a thing. But then, that wasn't my business.

"Are you ready to go home?" Harlow's voice broke through my thoughts and I turned to look at her. Her tired smile was a sign of a hard day working in the front while I was in the office doing all the paperwork. "Jaci and Aggie will take over for the last hour and make sure the doors are locked when they go home."

I liked how much trust we both had in our employees, and how much fun they had working for us. It made everything so much easier.

I got up from my chair and walked over to her, wrapping my arms around her waist and pulling her close. I lowered my lips to hers so kiss her.

"I'm ready," I told her between our kisses, and she smiled brightly, running her hands through my hair. "Good, because I think tonight's the right time."

I knew exactly what she meant, and I felt the same way. We might've been moving too quickly through our whole relationship, but we were ready. Ready for us to grow even more as a couple and a family.

Acknowledgements

Yet again, I want to thank Limitless Publishing for this opportunity. It's still a little surreal to me to be able to hold a paperback of my book in my hands and not just staring at it through my laptop screen. A big thank you to my editor Toni. Not sure how you made it through my first book without going crazy because it's been a wild one.

To Carolina Garza and Kerrie Manning: You two are incredible. Even if we only just started talking, I can't express how much gratitude I feel towards you. You've read Hunter when it was still on Wattpad. Thank you for supporting me from day one.

About The Author

Vanessa Siena is a twenty-something-year-old student with Italian roots living in Switzerland, where she was born and raised. Spending most of her free time as a teenager writing, she one day decided to upload her first official work "HUNTER" on Wattpad, where she reached over 100'000 reads in less than five months. When she's not writing, she plays bass guitar, reads novels and likes to eat to pass the time. Being very inspired by the '80s, rock bands from that time are always playing in the background.

Social Media Links

Instagram:
https://www.instagram.com/authorvanessasiena/

Wattpad:
https://www.wattpad.com/user/harlovv

Join our Reader Group on Facebook and don't miss out on meeting our authors and entering epic giveaways!

Limitless Reading

Where reading a book
is your first step to becoming
limitless...

LIMITLESS ◆ PUBLISHING *Reader Group*

Join today! *"Where reading a book is your first step to becoming limitless..."*

https://www.facebook.com/groups/LimitlessReading/

www.ingramcontent.com/pod-product-compliance
Lightning Source LLC
Chambersburg PA
CBHW020411210626
46816CB00006BB/2235